MW01241280

CRUMPLED PAPERS AND EMPTY CASKETS

AN ANTHOLOGY

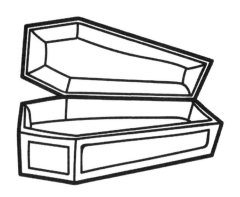

EDITED BY EMMA JANE LOUNSBURY

This book is a work of fiction. Names, characters, places, and incidents are the product of the author's imagination. Any resemblance to actual events, locales, or persons, living or dead, is coincidental.

Copyright © 2023

All rights reserved. No portion of this book may be reproduced in any form (other than for review purposes) without written permission from the publisher or author, except as permitted by U.S. copyright law. Each author is the sole copyright owner of their respective and individual Work, and retains all rights to the Work.

Paperback: 979-8-9889348-1-3

Ebook: 979-8-9889348-0-6

First edition October 2023

Edited by Emma Jane Lounsbury and Maddi Leatherman of EJL Editing

Cover art by Luke Reynolds

Formatted by Ciar Pfeffer

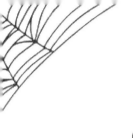

Table of Contents

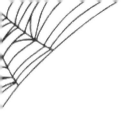

Foreword

by Maddi Leatherman

T he following collection of stories contains terrors that should not call these pages home, let alone this realm. Insidious tension drips from the words resting in your hands.

Already, you may feel the heavy gaze of unseen eyes resting between your shoulder blades. Slick tendrils of the unknown creep past your defenses, and cloying anxiety settles beneath your breastbone. Any lingering shred of peace decays until only one thing may reside within.

Fear.

Fear will play spectacular tricks on the mind. The brain resting in your skull is fickle and susceptible to forces of the unknown. Try as they might, the firing neurons within cannot always pinpoint reality. The desperate whirring of the mind triggers your baser instincts—fight or flight. Panic-induced hallucinations and catastrophized thoughts convince you that your dark demise lurks just around the corner.

So, dear reader, before continuing, ask yourself—what will you do when the writhing apparitions of your nightmares become reality?

The pages within unspool horrors, mysteries, and darkness. The confines of your covers will not be enough to protect you.

For hidden in the shadows, malevolence infiltrates and stalks the innocent. Cheerful faces mask cruel intentions. The final shreds of sanity slip beyond reach, and dark magic puppeteers the unsuspecting.

Of course, it's all a work of fiction. Stories spun to send shivers down your spine.

The tapping against your window? Merely the wind keeping time with the branches of the trees. A heavy thud in the attic? Surely, a box was once balanced too precariously atop forgotten memories, and a scampering mouse finally sent it crashing down. That tuneless humming that reverberates through the walls? A neighbor enjoying a late-night stroll on the sidewalk below, or more likely, an indication that your heating needs repairing.

Only, no brittle branches quite reach your window, do they? The attic collects dust, not boxes. The heater was replaced last year, and your only neighbors are well past eighty and drifted to sleep hours ago.

There is always a rational explanation. There is always the truth. What humans try desperately to ignore, however, is that rationality and truth might not always align.

You may choose to join the majority and turn your gaze from the fantastical. You may rewrite the narrative, straining to force logic into a box meant for madness.

But with each lie you tell yourself, that nagging fear will only grow more insistent. Your rationale will crumple into piles of discarded words. At the end of the day, you will step back and find your box is an empty casket beckoning you into its dark shadows.

To those who dare wander past this page, be forewarned: not all who venture into the darkness may cross back into the light.

A Note to the Reader

The stories in this collection are intended for mature readers. Some may warrant content and/or trigger warnings. These warnings can be found on the title page of each story.

Proceed at your own risk.

Absolution

Brig Berthold

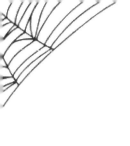

I needed to haul a load of lumber between Asheville and Knoxville, and my boss had been all over my ass about being on time. The shipment was due by dawn, and the sun's brief appearance on the horizon had long passed. Construction on the main freeway meant I would be late and being late meant losing my job. The adrenaline of fear buzzed through me, and I decided to take a two-lane, back road shortcut through the mountains. I figured it would be fine, but I was wrong.

Hours later, I rounded a curve, hugging the mountainside. A weight tugged at my eyelids until I let myself indulge in a slow blink. It couldn't have been long, no more than two or three seconds. I never saw the minivan. Its horn startled me awake. I corrected before I drove my truck off the side of the highway.

A resounding crash was audible over the sound of my air brakes. I pulled over and turned on my emergency flashers, grabbed a headlamp I sometimes used for repairs, and jumped from my rig. The other vehicle's horn was held down, echoing through the ravine. I followed the flattened roadside brush and found the car buried in a copse of trees. The engine block was wrapped around an oak like a deranged art project. My mind raced, repeating the word *no* over and over. I could tell the minivan was old. Looking through the open window, I was surprised there were no airbags. A dark-haired woman was slumped against the steering wheel, tears caught in her lifeless, blue eyes. Blood covered what I could see of her face, flowing from a terrible gash splitting her forehead.

I followed a hole in the windshield to a man's body, bent at odd angles, hanging in the split of a tree trunk. My body went cold at the shock.

A whimper came from the rear of the minivan. That's when I saw him. A freckle-faced teenage boy. Part of his head flattened against a splintered, tinted window. "Please," he whispered. The light from my headlamp glinted off his braces. "Please, God. Please." I watched him die—it took only a moment. There was nothing I could have done.

Standing there, fear gripped me. I was afraid to call the police. Afraid to lose my job. More than anything, I could not imagine explaining this to my wife, Claire. So, I didn't. I looked around at the still-empty highway and made my choice. Hurrying up the ravine, I climbed into my rig and drove away. A dark, empty feeling overtook me. It felt as if my soul had escaped, replaced by a vast emptiness. I remember asking myself what I'd done. I had killed that family. I had fallen asleep and killed them. And I never told a soul.

That was five years ago. For five years I've been coming to church every Sunday. Every week I silently beg for forgiveness. And every week, I feel no absolution. Does prayer count for nothing? Are my sins unforgivable?

The service was raving. Music spewed out of the amplifiers and drum kit. Members of the congregation raised their voices in song, praising Jesus, and speaking in tongues. A sweaty humidity hung in the air and rattled every part of my body. The rhythmic chaos, usually uplifting, devolved into a pounding distraction. The room's energy shifted as I realized God's spirit had left this meeting. Something had taken its place.

I noticed a cluster of wood and wire screen boxes on a low table at the foot of the stage that I'd never seen before. "Ali-kakalu," I heard and glanced up to the left of the stage at Sister Mary Strickland, her arms thrust into the air, head tilted toward God as she spoke in tongues. "Tomba gatu li li kakalu."

After fifty years on this earth, I knew only one thing for certain—I knew God lived. But in that moment, I knew He was no longer with us. The God whom I felt refused to forgive me still made His presence known to me. As though He still pursued me, inviting me to seek Him in return. He cleared my heart, allowing me to sense, more than see, the change.

I have been sensitive to darkness, both spiritual and physical, for these five years. I know when God is in the room because of the separation I feel from His love. Even as Mary's husband, Clive, continued his sermon, that feeling grew.

Clive and I had been friends since I moved here and joined this church. With all the time I spent on the road, it reassured me to have a friend like him. He was asked to preach occasionally, and I knew what it meant to him. Today, his words humbled me toward repentance, as though he had written the sermon for me.

"Brothers and sisters, God does not want us to live in sin. He asks very little of us when viewed from His eternal perspective. Repentance is the key to the Kingdom of God. What seems, to us, insurmountable, is but a pebble for Him."

Church had been an obligation after I married Claire. Since the accident, it was a personal requirement.

"Amen!" My wife's voice raised in exclamation. She returned my gaze, checking in on my fervor. I gave what I hoped was a reassuring smile. One corner of her mouth turned up, and she shook her head before she shifted her eyes back to the front of the chapel.

Clive Strickland held one hand in the air. He moved forward as though in a trance, his feet gliding along the stage. His eyes were as wide as semi-truck tires. Clive reached down, unclasped one of the boxes, and came up with a four-foot rattlesnake.

This was my first time seeing snakes in a church service and the feeling of separation from God began to make sense. I turned to my wife, needing to see whether she felt the same way. I flinched as shock crawled up my spine. A woman with dark hair turned to face me. The gash in her forehead was visible above her pale and bloody face. Her blue eyes glimmered back at me. I blinked and shook my head.

The dead woman was gone, leaving only my wife and her worried look. Claire leaned toward me, grabbed my arm, and I stooped down to hear her. "This is our way," she said. "I'm glad you finally get to experience this." She released her grip, and I returned my eyes to the stage.

I'd heard of snake handling, of course, but had always considered it local folklore. Was this actually happening?

Clive held the snake as its tail shook. Somehow, the sound of its rattle cut through the din. Its head danced in the air like an arrowhead. The tongue slid from its slim mouth, tasting the air. It was the color of sand with uneven triangular markings along its back. The beast bunched itself in Brother Strickland's hands.

The triumphant warrior of God, Clive turned the snake toward him. My heart raced as the two stared at one another, the snake's tongue darting in and out. My friend was drunk with the spirit—intoxicated by the power he held over this deadly proof of holiness. Clive's mouth opened as he began to shout in the name of God, commanding the poisonous serpent to be still in Jesus's name. He called out saying, "Jesus will judge mankind in His time and in His way."

"Bring me the spirit," he cried out above the rest of the noise. "I invite the spirit into my soul."

I saw the snake's head lash forward, its lower jaw separating from the base of its skull as it sunk its fangs into Clive's open cheek. Had I not been watching so closely, I'd have missed it.

The spell was broken and the congregation seemed to lunge forward all at once to help. Clive dropped the serpent, and a few of the men rushed to contain it. Someone picked up the snake by its tail and placed it back into the box, fastening the clasp.

Clive's hand was at his cheek, already beginning to swell. Mary Strickland rushed to her husband's side.

"Baby, let me call the ambulance," Mary said.

"Don't," Clive replied. "No doctors. I don't need them."

"But honey—"

"You heard what I said, Mary. If it's God's will that I die, so be it. At least it will have been in His name, caught up in His spirit, praising Him."

"Praise Jesus," Mary said.

"Hallelujah," my wife said.

"I believe in you, Clive," I said.

"Don't believe in me. Believe in God. Pray for His will to be done and the strength to stand tall, no matter what He decides."

I converted to this church ten years ago. I spent my childhood attending various church services with friends when I'd stay over during weekends. They were all Christians, and I'd learned about Jesus, in my own way, and my own time. In the years before my conversion, there was an emptiness in my life where God should be.

When Claire and I eventually married, joining her family's church was expected. So, I converted. But I never shook off the feeling that I was considered an interloper. Accepted, but not among, and to be honest, I didn't really care. But after the accident, I knew I needed God.

Clive was a convert as well and had also married into the faith and the community. That brought us together. Our families had all been close and had spent a lot of time with each other.

"Hey, are you okay?" my wife asked me.

All day I was lost in thought. I couldn't get Clive and Mary off my mind. Something gnawed at me and wouldn't leave me alone.

"Hmm," I grunted. "I'm fine. Just thinking about Clive. Hope he's okay."

"I've been thinking about them, too. I'll call Mary and see how they're doing."

Claire made the call. From the side of the conversation I could hear, it sounded like Mary denied visits or support. Claire hung up.

"She said they're fine." Claire let out a breath. "But I don't know how you could be after that." Worry overtook her.

I nodded, chewing the inside of my lip.

"Why don't you go over?" she said. "Just a quick visit. Check in on them and see what we can do to help."

"Now?"

"Yes, now," she said.

"And why am I going alone?"

"Because," Claire said, "I have to finish baking a cake for the youth activity tomorrow."

I shuffled to my feet and grabbed my keys.

Before I left the house, Claire called out, "You be careful. It'll be late when you get there, and you know how I feel about driving at night."

I knew better than she ever would. Shaking off the feeling, I fired up my pickup and headed up the mountain.

L eaves burned orange and red as if in defiance of the inevitable death winter would bring. Despite the air's cold snap, I had my window down. I especially appreciated the breaks in trees giving me glimpses over the tops of the tree line. Soon, sunset would burn off the final moments of the day.

The poorly maintained road rumbled beneath my pickup. Though I had driven this route many times, the narrow lanes made me tense, straining around curves, relaxing into straight-aways, climbing the mountain all the way.

The higher up the mountain I climbed, the more civiliza-tion gave way to nature's impressive persistence. Rounding one curve, I looked out over the town. The steeples of three promi-nent churches were the only signs of humanity. White needles poked through the foliage as though God looks more favorably upon those more visible from Heaven.

Something was bothering me, but I couldn't figure out what it was. My feelings stood in contrast to the beauty around me. I'd seen my friend bitten by a snake earlier. That was unnerving, but some part of me knew that wasn't the only thing upsetting me. The further I drove, the closer I got to labeling the feeling. And yet, it seemed to avoid being caught, staying just out of reach.

Clouds swallowed up the ridgeline, capturing the last of the sunset. Wind kicked up leaves along the forest floor as I drove my truck down the narrow dirt path. Two grooves carved into the earth created a one-way lane to the Strickland's trailer. Trees overhung the property and waved with each gust of wind.

The yard was littered with bent aluminum lawn chairs, a flat-tired bicycle, and other long-abandoned bits of life. A weathered plank of particleboard covered the nearest window and a faint glow of light shone around the uneven edges.

I eased off the lane and parked on the grass beside Clive's pickup. Pulling out my phone, I texted Claire to let her know I was safe. An error indicated the message didn't send. The icon where service bars should be showed only a satellite and the letters *SOS*. I cursed, slipped the phone back into my pocket, and slid down out of my truck.

Despite the wind, the air was stale, as though the holler itself refused to accept outside influence. Between the truck and the trailer, I paused a moment. Something dark rolled around in my chest. I thought of the church service and my awareness of God's sudden departure. I had that feeling again, standing in front of my friend's home. Cautiously, I moved forward. And I prayed. I reached for the door and knocked.

A skittering sound came from behind the door, as though my knock startled some creature from its hiding place. Shifting my weight, I knocked again. This time, I heard whispers on the other side of the door. It sounded like an argument.

"Clive?" I raised my voice to be heard through the door. "Mary? It's Bill Walsh. I came to check on you."

The whispering stopped—cut off. "Bill," I heard then, "it's awful nice of you to stop by, but we're doing just fine. Thank you, kindly."

It sounded like Mary, almost. Her voice was strangled, and if I wasn't worried before, I was then.

"Mary, what's going on in there?"

"Nothing, Bill. Like I said, everything's fine."

"Well, how's Clive? Claire and I are worried."

"It's just you?" she asked.

"Yeah. Mary, what's going on?"

From behind the door came another burst of whispers, sharper this time. The sound of a deadbolt knocked against the door and then it creaked open. Mary stood halfway behind the door, her bowed head was wrapped in a scarf of some kind. She would not meet my eye.

A breath of concern passed through me. I entered the trailer, thanking Mary for letting me in.

"You're welcome," she said and then choked.

Mary had always been thin, the way some folks' lives are too much working and not enough eating. I flushed with embarrassment as I saw she wore only her nightshirt. She kept her eyes fixed near my feet as she shut the door behind me. I noticed she threw the deadbolt again.

The front of the trailer was lit with a dim, yellow glow. A dining room to the right of the entryway was decorated with a cheap table, surrounded by mismatched chairs. A bulky chandelier hung from the ceiling and swayed gently, as though blown by a breeze. To the left was a kitchen, and a bar separated it from the entryway.

The carpet was somewhere between mud and dried blood-colored and ran down a narrow hallway toward the back of the double-wide. Tongue and groove pine boards lacquered the color of honey oak wrapped around the walls, occasionally broken up by the odd picture frame hanging askew.

The evening chill outside was warmer than this. I shivered where I stood. The thermostat must have been turned down as low as it would go.

"Well, Mary. Where's Clive?"

Mary turned, and rather than speak, her hand rose and pointed down the hall toward the back of the trailer.

"Mary, what's wrong? Are you okay?" I reached out and Mary twisted away from me. She shuffled toward the kitchen. I didn't know what was going on, but something was wrong. I was interrupted before I could press for an answer.

"Who's there?" Clive hollered from down the hall.

The family's living room was at the back of the trailer.

"It's Bill Walsh, Clive," I called back.

"Bill?" Clive sounded as if he'd belched while saying my name. "What're you doing here?"

"I come to check on you and Mary." I paused, disturbed by the faint puff of steam my words produced in the cold air. "We're worried about you."

"Come on back."

I moved slowly, cautioned by the growing sense of wrongness. An earthy, musky smell tickled my nose. The smell grew stronger the further down the hall I moved.

The back of the trailer was dark, lit only by a pale blue light, flickering occasionally. I realized it must have been the television flashing between scenes. Oddly, there was no noise in the otherwise black room.

It was colder in the living room, and the darkness of it matched my feelings. The television flickered again, showing Clive seated in his easy chair. My friend reached up and turned on a lamp set on an end table beside him. Thumbing the remote, he turned off the television.

The dim, yellow glow showed Clive's face had swollen far beyond where the snake had bitten him. Half of his face seemed twice its normal size. A mass of black spread across his mouth like rancid barbeque sauce. The discoloration spiderwebbed like veins from ear to ear, stopping just beneath his eyes. His skin the color of storm-gray clouds.

Clive's eyes had always been a jovial green and would light up at the sight of you. Now, all I could see were sockets of black, glistening obsidian. The dark feeling grew in my chest, and a heaviness rested on my shoulders.

I glanced away, trying to mask my horror. Like the hallway, the living room was lined with pine tongue and groove panels, the carpet a deep emerald green. Stained clothing, takeout containers, and all manner of filth covered every available surface. The smell assaulted me. That same musky smell, like a rat's nest, floated overtop a potent mix of body odor and something metallic. Copper?

"How are you?" Clive said, sounding as though he spoke through cotton balls. He made no effort to stand.

"Fine," I said. "How are you?" I forced myself to face him again.

My friend smiled then, and I couldn't escape the thought that he delighted in my lie. I was the furthest thing from fine.

Clive cocked his head to the left. He surveyed me the way a dog examines an odd sound.

"You don't seem fine, Bill. I'd say you haven't been fine for years. Can we finally talk about that?" Clive's words sounded obstructed, caught in a pneumonia-like phlegm.

I mustered my courage and turned to face him, or it, or whatever my friend had become. I saw the glint in his black eyes. I felt more alone than on that empty highway. Clive waved me toward him. Without a word, he indicated to the seat across from him, the palm of his hand open in invitation.

My feet sounded like sandpaper as I shuffled along the carpet. I was wary of the upward turn at the corner of Clive's mouth and the blackened skin folding in on itself.

I sat in the chair facing Clive's and shivered, wrapping my arms around myself. I found my voice, "We've been worried about you—"

"You said that, already. I want to know why you've come. Why you're really here." He paused to cough into a handkerchief already balled into his fist. When he stopped, the fabric came away darker than blood.

"Like I said, I'm here to—"

"Don't give me that Boy Scout bullshit," Clive said, cutting me off again. "This isn't some rescue mission. You're not here because of some outreach project. But you convinced yourself it was, didn't you?"

I wondered what the hell I was supposed to say to that.

"You're here because I summoned you, Billy."

The words came unlike any I'd heard before. High-pitched and reedy but choked, garbled but succeeding through the strain.

"Clive?" I said aloud. My breathing increased through the shock.

"He can't hear you. Not unless I allow it."

Eyes wide with confusion, I stared at my friend. His head lolled to one side as black drool escaped the side of his mouth.

"Clive!" I shouted. "What is happening, Clive?"

Light returned to those black eyes as his head righted itself. My friend's mouth opened but that strange voice came from it. "I told you, Billy." He said my name with derision. "Clive can't hear you. He's not here. It's just you and me."

"Mary," I yelled. Turning toward the hallway, I pushed myself out of the chair. The sensation of half a dozen hands gripped me from all sides. The hands pulled me backward, spun me around, and forced me back into the chair.

A gravelly, disembodied laugh came from Clive's mouth. "I'm in charge, here."

The hands released their grip on me. "What do you want?"

"Billy, don't you want to know who I am first?"

"I don't care who you are."

"Such bravery."

"I know you," I said. My voice shook with fear and cold. "I know you well enough."

The thing smiled, "We've met, though not formally. The family in the trees on the side of the highway. The glorious sounds of broken bone and twisted metal. I can still taste the blood from that woman's face. I remember watching your fear turn cold as you ran, Billy. Do you remember? Do you still see them? Does that boy still whisper to you?"

I bit back the emotion. My fear turned to familiar grief, and I dropped my eyes.

"So, you do remember," it said to me. "I was pleased with you that night."

"Get out of my head." I rocked back and forth in my chair.

"It wasn't long after that you started driving a truck, was it? An excuse to leave. Who could have stopped you? Escape never felt so good, did it?"

"What do you want, demon?"

"That's a step in the right direction. Respect. I like that."

The demon was right. Truck driving wasn't the only thing in my life that changed back then. I also found God and gave my life to Jesus. I shut my eyes and tried to focus on the joy God had brought into my life. I began to pray, *Lord Jesus, deliver me from the hands of this evil*.

"There is no saving you, Billy. Stop embarrassing yourself."

Prayer continued spilling from my mouth in whispered gasps.

"You believe all that shit, don't you?"

"I am prepared for you, demon. I have the shield of faith and the sword of the Spirit. And with the word of God, I will deliver this family from you." Though I trembled with fear, I sensed the power in my words. The weight behind them gave me strength.

I opened my eyes and glared into the demon's vacant sockets. "Leave this place in the name of God," I blurted. "The power of Christ compels you."

Laughter rang out as though the walls were filled with mirth. The roots of my teeth vibrated and began to itch.

"That never gets old. I saw that film too, you know."

The demon extended his hand toward the floor. A snake began working its way up Clive's arm, twisting itself as it slithered past the shoulder and behind my friend's neck. It settled into a gently writhing shawl. The demon reached a hand up and stroked the snake—a lover's caress.

I glanced around and, for the first time, noticed the snakes silently slipping in and out of the room's filth. I heard a rattle below me as a snake curled itself around my left ankle. Its head was back, like a taut string, rattling its warning.

When the demon spoke again, its voice held more weight and menace. "Your friend invited me, but I've been wanting to visit with you for some time."

"I have nothing to say to you, beast."

"Are you afraid yet, Billy?"

I shrank back, clenching my eyes shut, feeling defeated. When I opened my eyes, I saw Clive's green eyes glimmering back at me.

"Don't leave me, Bill."

I sat up, eyes wide. It was Clive's voice. My friend spoke to me.

"Bill, help me," he said. His words were strained with effort and pain. But it was Clive, there was no doubt about that. "I'm fighting him. I'm fighting, but I can't fight for long. Get out of here, Bill. You have to leave. It's too strong."

I stood and took a half-step toward my friend. I'd forgotten the snake wrapped around my ankle until the beads rattled in its tail.

"Clive, I can help. Tell me what to do. Tell me what it wants."

"Mary," Clive called out. His tone was a mix of anger and desperation. "Mary!"

Mary ran into the room. Her bare feet were visible beneath the hem of her white nightshirt. "Clive? Clive, are you all right?" She failed to muffle the sobs behind her words.

She rushed to Clive's side, and I watched as she grabbed the rattlesnake from around his neck. She whipped the creature backward and the snake flew across the room with a thud onto the floor. Mary grabbed Clive around the neck, hugging him. "Baby, you're back. Thank you, Jesus."

"No. Mary. Leave—" Clive managed to say before his words were cut off.

"He is not here." It was the demon's voice again. Clive's eyes had receded into blackness.

To my horror, Mary rose into the air. She floated as if held by some unseen tether. Her feet kicked, searching for the floor two feet beneath her. She screamed. The demon made Clive's body smile, showing decayed teeth.

"Stop," I said. "Leave her alone."

"She will pay for her sins. You all will." Clive's body sat up. No longer was he crumpled into his easy chair.

The snakes hissed around the room as if celebrating the moment. I turned back at a sharp crack. The bones in her right arm snapped between her wrist and elbow. Her cries became something else. Something otherworldly. One by one, the demon snapped the bones in Mary's body.

"You like that, Billy?"

I turned toward the demon who stared right at me. Tears coated my face. I couldn't keep watching, but unseen hands grabbed my head and turned it toward Mary. A final snap and the sounds of Mary's pain died with her, leaving only my sobs. A sound like a loose sack of apples being dropped came as she was released onto the floor.

"Shut up, you. Stop your blubbering. She had it coming."

"Why?" I said in a whisper.

"Come on, Billy. I thought you'd appreciate seeing what a shattered body looks like again."

"What are you talking about?" Bile burned my throat as it rose from my stomach. I knew. I had tried to forget. Tried for five years to run from that moment—to bury it in life.

"You must pay for your sins, Billy." The demon smiled at me. "You won't miss it this time, Billy. I won't let you miss a thing. And when we're done here, you're coming with me. I think your wife needs to know what kind of man she married."

"No!"

"You thought you could simply repent, and everything would be okay."

The demon laughed.

My awareness came and went as we drove down the mountain. One moment I gripped the steering wheel, and the next, I was buried inside myself. I felt shackled. Chained, somehow, to that empty space where my soul once was. The demon was strong, and there was barely enough room for both of us. It pressed against me, drowning me, suffocating my consciousness. I fought, pushing and pulling my way out until I retook control.

The truck raced down the narrow mountain road, moving too fast. My headlights lit up the double yellow line as the truck swayed between both lanes. The brakes felt stiff beneath my foot. As the demon attacked my mind from within, I worked to sort through my thoughts.

"It won't work, Billy."

"Get out of my head."

"You can't win."

The shadows of trees rushed by as the truck rounded a curve. Momentum pulled us to one side and the tires strained to stay on the road. Quickly, the road straightened out, and we tipped back into place.

Fire burned behind my eyes as sharp pain knifed through my head. The demon's voice echoed in me.

"I can't wait to see Claire. To tell her she's married to a murderer. Her last moments will be filled with betrayal and fear."

I was losing control. It was too strong. I would have prayed, but knew it would do no good. God had abandoned me years ago. Visions of the accident came back into my mind, and I felt the demon's glee at my remembering. The man's mangled corpse. The woman's bloody face. The boy's final plea.

"I won't let you win," I said. I spoke aloud and felt part of my mouth was numb. It nearly had me. This was it.

"You have no choice, Billy. I always win."

What little light I could see from the headlights started to dim. I still had control of my limbs even as I lost everything else. I pressed down on the accelerator and gripped the steering wheel. Ahead, yellow signs indicated a curve in the road.

"Not this time," I said.

We slammed into the dirt built up along the road's edge. I thought of Claire as weightlessness brought an empty tickle to my stomach. We left the pavement. I told myself I was protecting her. Branches whipped the sides of the truck, and the mountain fell away beneath us.

About the Author

B rig is a veteran of the war in Afghanistan and an alumni member of the Wounded Warrior Project. Following a military career, he earned a degree in journalism. Brig is also co-host of the Baseball Together Podcast, bringing fans weekly discussion and analysis to a worldwide audience. He believes the best way to do baseball is together. He is currently enjoying the short story form, exploring both genre and thematic limits while he pursues a Master of Fine Arts degree. He lives in South Carolina with his fiancé, two seven-year-old girls, and their Rottweiler.

Whispers from the Veil

Nelle Nikole

Warning:

Based on True Events

Proceed with Caution

To the eternal traveler,

Within the following pages, you will embark on a journey into the chilling realm of the supernatural. Be forewarned that the tales you are about to encounter are not mere works of fiction but are rooted in the bone-chilling reality of true events.

Ghosts, malevolent entities, and unexplainable phenomena lurk in the shadows, eager to seize your imagination and awaken your deepest fears. As you delve deeper into these narratives, remember that the line between the living and the dead is often thinner than we dare to imagine.

The story contained herein is inspired by the experiences of someone who has glimpsed the other side, who has encountered the inexplicable, and who has grappled with the paranormal. These encounters have left an indelible mark on their soul yet they find themself brave enough to share it, and now, it will leave a mark on you.

But heed this warning: spirits do not always play by the rules, and their presence is not to be taken lightly. They are a testament to the enduring mysteries of our world and the enduring fear of the unknown.

As you turn the pages, be prepared for your beliefs to be tested, your courage to be questioned, and your nights to be filled with lingering shadows. This story is not for the faint of heart, and once you step into this world, there may be no turning back.

So, my dear reader and spooky soul, proceed with caution.

May you find your way back from the other side unscathed, but know that the echoes of these true events will haunt you long after the final page has been turned.

With trepidation and anticipation,

Nelle Nikole

When I was just a little girl, people always told me ghosts weren't real. They said what I'd seen was merely a figment of my imagination. The sounds I heard at night were the TV, and when I would wake up in front of the window with no knowledge of how I'd gotten there, it was dismissed as sleepwalking.

I was a fool to believe that.

Before my family moved into that old house in a small, backwoods town in Virginia, things had never felt right inside. It's all too easy to dismiss things when you're a kid—swift shadows moving across your bedroom wall, toys appearing in places you hadn't left them, and imaginary friends that felt a bit too real.

It wasn't until I got older that I realized one thing; imaginary friends are never imaginary.

Most children outgrow their imaginary friends, losing the sensitive connection to the other side as they go through life and establish their own belief systems. That never happened for me. Instead, they became fixtures in my life, presenting themselves where I least expected it.

Winchester, Virginia had seen its share of history. The Shenandoah Valley was a fruitful place for trading and hunting for members of the Shawnee and Cherokee tribes. Then European settlers arrived, and the familiar story unfolded. Guns, germs, and glory. Soon enough, the indigenous people were gone, replaced by plantations and settlers. That era ended with the Civil War, and my home sat right on the battlefields, like many others around us.

Land remembers the injustices that memory cannot. History is written by the victors after all. It's still their land. The final resting places to their cruel demise—whether the past is acknowledged or not.

I guess I shouldn't have been shocked the first time I woke up paralyzed, a dark figure looming over me, watching. There had been signs before that.

I never liked scary movies, but my mother was a fanatic. I usually skipped out, preferring not to indulge my sensitivity to the other side. When we first moved into that cursed home, my brother's toys would activate, their batteries removed, yet still, sounds emanated from them. Everyone would shrug it off, but it always gave me a peculiar feeling—a twisted, fluttering sensation in the pit of my stomach, the kind that triggers your fight-or-flight response. But I kept quiet; I didn't want to be dismissed again.

When I turned fifteen, the voices started. Laughter and background noise, mostly. I would wake up around 3 a.m. to it every night—the witching hour, as my friends teased. My father was a gamer and a night owl, often requiring very little sleep. It wasn't uncommon for him to be up playing games into the early hours of the morning. Unfortunately, I was a light sleeper, needing absolute silence to rest properly. The walls of that old Virginia

CRUMPED PAPERS AND EMPTY CASKETS

home were paper thin. One night, I mustered the courage to confront my mother about it, asking her and my father to keep it down after my brother and I had gone to bed.

My mother gave me a concerned look, brushing my long black hair behind my ear. "Sweetie, your father and I have been going to bed early since we moved in. I'm not sure what you're hearing, but you've always been an active sleeper. Just try to ignore it."

It was the same dismissal I'd always received, so I kept quiet over the months that followed. I felt crazy, like I was losing my mind in a family with a history of mental illness. My dogs began to sleep with me, trying to bring me comfort, but there was none to be found. Instead, they woke up at the same time, growling into the dark corners of my room.

I reached my breaking point months later, unable to bear the fear that crept up my spine, paralyzing me under the covers and clutching my heart. Cautiously, I began to bring my fears to my mother's attention with each bump in the night, but her response remained the same: they were in bed, and as far as they knew, the house remained quiet.

My friend Hadley had been the only one to take me seriously. "There's a thin veil between this world and the next, you know," she cautioned. "The more you entertain them, the more they'll reach out."

I stared at her, my lunch growing cold and unappetizing in front of me. It was the next day during lunch period. Our high school's cafeteria around us seemed to fade into the background as her words hung in the air, heavy and foreboding.

"How do I stop it?" I asked, my voice barely a whisper, as if speaking any louder would invite the very darkness I feared.

Hadley leaned in closer, her eyes darting around as if she were afraid even the walls had ears. "You can't stop it completely," she admitted, her voice barely audible. "But you can try to set boundaries, protect yourself. Try to ask them to stop."

A chill crept down my spine as her words painted a picture of a world teetering on the edge of the unknown. The air in the cafeteria seemed to grow colder, and I could feel unseen eyes upon us, watching, waiting.

Hadley continued, her tone urgent, "Salt, iron, sage—these can offer some protection. But you have to be firm, unwavering. Never invite them in willingly. Don't acknowledge their presence unless you have to."

I nodded, my heart pounding in my chest. The surrounding noise, the clatter of trays and chatter of students, seemed distant, as if we were in our own isolated bubble of fear. I trusted her advice. Maybe it was silly, but Hadley was obsessed with all things spooky. If there was anyone to know about this kind of thing, it'd be her.

"And whatever you do," Hadley whispered, her eyes locked onto mine, "never, ever say their name out loud. It gives them power, a foothold in our world."

"I don't know their name. I don't even know what *they are*," I muttered, more to myself than her.

"Good," Hadley said, seemingly satisfied. "Keep it that way."

I felt a shiver run through me as I absorbed her words. The thin veil between the living and the dead suddenly seemed suffocatingly thin, and I couldn't shake the feeling that something malevolent lurked just beyond it, waiting for any opportunity to break through.

Hadley's warning had cast a shadow over my world, one that I couldn't ignore. The world around us remained oblivious to my fear, but for me, the boundary between reality and the supernatural had blurred irreversibly, and I knew that I had to tread carefully in the ever-darkening waters of the paranormal.

At this point, I had nothing left to lose, so reaching out and asking them to stop seemed like my best bet. But it didn't work.

After a year of torment, I began to sleep with the television on, attributing every chuckle, voice, footstep, or murmur to whatever show was playing in the background. I was seriously starting to consider the fact that I may be schizophrenic. Telling my parents what was going on was fruitless, and the last thing I wanted to do was be dragged back to therapy.

My room was all the way across the house from my parents, separated by a long bridge and several walls. It was painted a beautiful shade of purple, with furniture from the previous owners that had a beautiful Victorian aesthetic matching the outside of the house. It was stunning during the day, peaceful even. But at night, it came alive.

A dark oak bookcase stretched along the wall adjacent to my bed, leaving a small gap in the corner. It was just big enough for a small child, like my brother. One night, I heard incessant scratching from the dark abyss. My dogs went berserk, barking and howling, their bodies tense and ready to defend. My room was so separated from everyone else that I knew no one would be coming to help. I was starting to feel really stupid for thinking the distance would give me "privacy."

I found myself frozen with fear, staring into the corner, trying to figure out if something was actually there. When I realized that the courage to investigate or flee would never come, and the dogs eventually settled down, I turned up the volume on Disney Channel, and willed myself to go back to sleep.

For the next week, I heard the same scratching every night, like clockwork around 3 a.m. My dogs would sound off, barking and growling but carefully avoiding the corner, as if they, too, were afraid. They circled me protectively. I knew they were shielding me from whatever lurked there. Animals can see what eludes the human eye. The mind plays tricks on us, you see. Not cruel ones, but ones meant to protect us, to keep us sane.

I knew I'd be dismissed if I brought it to my mother's attention, but at some point, I stopped caring about sounding crazy and sought help where I knew I wouldn't find it.

Her excuse this time was new. "It's probably just the tree outside your room scraping against the wall."

From that point on, I made a mental note to keep my thoughts to myself. I was on my own.

Around the same time that the scratching began, I noticed that I would wake up and find myself standing, staring outside my window. I had always sleepwalked, but it was rare, usually involving me wandering into the kitchen to indulge in some late-night snacking. But this time was different. I always found myself in front of the window, fully dressed, gazing out onto the pitch-black street.

Apparently, people in Virginia did not believe in streetlights. Each time I awoke, I felt mentally exhausted, as if I had been fighting to regain control of my body and had won. It felt less and less like waking up from sleep and more like being jolted back into my body. Random bruises and cuts appeared on my legs and ribs. After this, facing myself in the mirror became impossible. I was scared to see what would confront me in my own reflection after the first time *it* touched me.

I'd been washing my face at the sink, tucked down and splashing the water up. I felt it then—a presence behind me that had fear racing through me. My heart pounded in my ears but I didn't want to face it. I refused to look up. Someone was standing behind me, I was sure of it. The refusal to acknowledge it seemed to anger it. Whatever it was, it wanted its presence known.

Thriving off my fear, it reached out and shoved me. My head collided with the faucet, leaving a knot in its place, but that wasn't what scarred me. No, it was the way I was forced to lie to everyone I knew that my migraines had taken a toll, and I'd passed out unexpectedly. But I knew the truth, knew that one day, if I couldn't control this, it would come for me and it would not be gentle.

H igh school turned into college, and I ventured far away from Virginia. I met my roommate, Ophelia, through Facebook, and we quickly became best friends. Her grandmother had passed away the summer before school started, so her room was covered in photos of the two of them. Funny enough, her grandmother hated taking pictures. Every time we left the dorm and returned, photos of her and her grandmother would be scattered on the ground, while the ones with her friends and other family members remained on the wall, untouched.

Not wanting to be the weird girl who believed in ghosts, I shrugged it off as nothing. After all, it was what I had run from—my sensitivity to the other side. "Here," I offered, bringing in some duct tape I'd used in my own room. "You're probably just not hanging them up right."

The next day, we returned from class, and every single photo of Ophelia's grandmother had fallen off the wall. It was both eerie and intriguing. To comfort myself, I told myself that my little ghost in Virginia was probably my own grandfather, simply playing pranks on me. He hadn't meant to harm me that day, only taken a joke a bit too far. I'd only met him a few times before he died, but I was always told he was quite the prankster.

Her grandmother's presence in the room was undeniable, as if she were trying to communicate from beyond the grave. Weeks went by, and strange things continued to happen. A roommate we'd known to be chill, that existed in a constant meditative state suddenly became extremely aggressive and broke down. She moved out a week later. Our third roommate soon followed in her footsteps. I remember watching her leave, the haunting, empty look in her eyes as she left without so much as a goodbye. We never got a real explanation for these events, but it was sudden and their behavior changed quickly, becoming uncharacteristic.

The next year, Ophelia, our friend, and I decided to room together in an apartment-style dorm. One night I was at work, a hostess at a popular nearby pub. It was slow at the restaurant, so I passed the time scrolling through scary stories on an iPad. It was out of character for me. I usually avoided such stories. But that night, temptation got the better of me, and it would turn out to be a grave mistake.

I arrived home before anyone else and decided to claim the first shower of the night while I could. As I stepped out, I opened the door to my room, and the fairy lights strung along the ceiling started to move like a jump rope—up, down, up, down. It resembled a snake slithering along my wall. I stood there, stunned, not wanting to believe my eyes. It wasn't until a poster on my wall ripped in half that I sprinted into the hallway, completely naked, my towel dropped back inside.

"Are you okay?" a guy in the hallway asked as he passed by, quickly removing his jacket and offering it to me to cover my body. My trembling fingers fumbled to accept the jacket, and my shivering form was concealed under its warmth.

Stuttering, I wasn't sure how to answer. What could I tell him? That my room was haunted? The paranormal is terrifying, but people can be cruel. The darkness that had unfolded before me still clung to my mind like a vise, its eerie grip refusing to loosen.

He grabbed my key from me, seeing the fear in my eyes, a fear that went beyond the chill in the air. "Let's get you back inside. You look like you've just seen a ghost," he teased, unaware of how true that statement was. His casual remark sent a shiver down my spine.

Since I was a naked girl in the hallway of a co-ed dorm, I told him I had actually seen a ghost. "Can you please come inside with me and look around while I get some clothes?" My voice quivered with both fear and urgency, my desperation for a feeling of safety overpowering my embarrassment.

He agreed, and I invited him in. The hallway felt like an impenetrable void, and my chances with Strangerman seemed infinitely better than whatever awaited me inside. He disappeared into the darkness of my bedroom, leaving me to anxiously await his return.

In the dimly lit living room, my boyfriend at the time appeared through the open dorm room door. The second I'd stepped inside, I sent a flurry of frantic texts begging him to come down. His stern expression conveyed his annoyance, unaware of the surreal terror that had just unfolded in the hallway.

"What's your problem?" Jace berated me, holding the door open for the other guy to leave. His eyes bore into mine, searching for an explanation.

Strangerman turned back to me sympathetically before departing. I never learned his name, but he was kind to me when I needed it the most, an unexpected source of comfort in my time of distress. He always said hello when I saw him around campus in the following years, asking if I was doing okay, a silent understanding passing between us.

"There's something here, Jace. I don't know what it is, but . . . I think it followed me from Virginia." My words were hesitant, as if merely uttering them would make the malevolent presence real once again.

"What are you talking about?" he said, slamming my poster back on the wall with a series of putties and duct tape. His tone was aggravated, making me feel like the act of fixing my room in an attempt to restore normalcy was an inconvenience.

I knew at that moment to shut up. I had learned over the years whom to trust and who would call me crazy. I sank onto my bed, the room now cloaked in an uneasy silence, as if the very walls held their breath, waiting for the next chilling revelation.

That night, I went to bed terrified. Surprisingly, I found myself having a pleasant dream when an old, ragged woman suddenly appeared.

"Watch out!" she screamed.

I shot up in bed just in time to see my closet door slam shut and the poster rip back off the wall. It was weeks before I felt comfortable sleeping in my room again. I rotated between sleeping on the floor in my roommates' rooms and the living room, yet the eerie feeling followed me no matter where I went.

Things at home began to unravel. An old clock with no batteries started working again, pumpkins melted on our front porch in forty-degree weather, black cats appeared from seemingly thin air. The paranormal are like fleas; if you see one, there's always more.

My mother had finally begun to come around, but religion clouded her judgment. She believed me, but only to a certain extent. A Bible arrived, and she instructed me to bless the place. At that point, religion and I had a complicated relationship. How could God protect me while I found myself repeatedly victimized by an unknown evil? Desperate for relief, I agreed, searching online for house blessing rituals and sleeping with the Bible on the shelf above my bed.

I worked hard to push all thoughts of the paranormal out of my head. As it turned out, Hadley had been right. Internet searches showed me that the more open I was to the other side, the more likely things were to reach out to me. That's what I had done that night when I searched for haunting tales on the iPad—I had exposed myself, and I felt like a fool.

Months went by after blessing my space and being intentional about what I allowed into my space. Unfortunately for me, I had traded one torment for another. My new boyfriend, Grant, insisted on watching *The Exorcism* despite my pleas. In the tizzy of the honeymoon phase, we had practically moved in together at that point, so instead of arguing with him about it, I decided to go to sleep while he watched.

Around 3 a.m., I woke up to the bedroom TV being launched off the wall, unplugging itself and crashing to the floor in front of the bed. He leaped out of bed, his eyes fixed on the door to the living room and the tv now on the floor.

"Did you open that?" he asked, his voice trembling, as he pointed to the half-cracked door.

I gave a nervous laugh. "No. Maybe you got up to use the bathroom and forgot to close it."

He shook his head, his eyes still glued to the dark gap. We both knew the answer to each other's questions; there was no way for either of us to get out of bed without disturbing the other. I was a notoriously light sleeper, waking up if someone passed by even in the hallway. If I got out of bed, I would have had to crawl over him to do so.

Guilt gnawed at me. I knew deep down that whatever had found me in that damned house in Virginia had followed me, and now it was affecting those around me. I had become a conduit for the darkness, and I didn't know how to rid myself of it.

I cleansed Grant's space, and we never spoke of it again.

Years passed. I graduated from college and was twenty-two, feeling invincible. You know, that sense of freedom after leaving academia made me believe I had the whole world at my feet. It had taken me years, but I had finally mastered the art of shielding myself from the other side within my home. At some point, I'd begun to find joy in being able to connect with that side when I pleased. After a while, I began to accept it for what it was—a gift.

Most people want to see into the other side, to experience a ghostly interaction just once as proof that life continues after death. But it was on a trip to Savannah, Georgia that I learned what I was truly dealing with. For a refreshing change of events, a supportive man entered my life. Joey was fairly religious and a skeptic, but respected my experiences and was open to seeing the truth for himself.

We decided to take a ghost tour. I'd taken one in the city before, which had its own horrors, but as it was one of my favorite cities to travel to, I typically found a new tour with each visit. The night was chilly and we couldn't have prepared enough for the drizzling rain and freezing temperatures.

We huddled together in the desolate corner of the park, shivering as the biting wind sliced through the darkness, and waited with bated breath for the tour guides to arrive. The night had grown colder, and the veil between the living and the dead seemed to thin with every passing moment. Shadows danced eerily under the flickering lampposts, creating a haunting backdrop for the unfolding events.

Then, like apparitions themselves, two sisters emerged from the dark corners of the park square, their presence an unsettling disturbance in the frigid air. They were not part of the scheduled tour, their arrival a twist of fate that still sends shivers down my spine at the thought.

"I'm sorry to say this to you, and please don't freak out, but we think you should know," one of the sisters spoke. Her voice quivered with an eerie resonance that seemed to echo with an otherworldly presence. A look of sorrow etched deep lines onto her face, as though she carried the weight of centuries-old secrets.

My heart quickened, dread settling in my chest, for I had already sensed the ominous revelation that awaited. "Excuse me?" I said nervously, already having a sense of what this was about. "Know what?"

My partner's grip tightened around my hand, an unspoken understanding passing between us.

The other sister stepped forward, her piercing gaze locking onto mine, sending shivers down my spine. "We think you should know because it's something you've suspected for a while now," she declared in a hushed tone, her words laden with an otherworldly weight. "I can feel it. There is something attached to you, and it has been for a long time. If it's okay with you, we'd like to cleanse you."

Stunned and unable to form coherent words, I simply nodded, my thoughts a whirlwind of fear, doubt, and anticipation. The air grew thick with an impending darkness, and I felt my body becoming a battleground, torn between surrendering to the cleansing and resisting the forces that sought to consume me.

"In nomine Patris, et Filii, et Spiritus Sancti," the sisters began in unison, their hands hovering over my body.

In mere minutes that felt like an eternity, I spiraled into a nightmarish abyss, losing myself in a maelstrom of thoughts and emotions. My very identity slipped away as I warred with the malevolent entity that clung to my soul.

And then, as swiftly as it began, it ended. I found myself standing on the precipice of sanity, my breaths ragged, and my heart pounding like a relentless drum. A suffocating weight had lifted from my chest, one that I had been carrying unknowingly for years.

They flipped through photos on a phone, revealing a photograph taken before they'd approached. Panic surged through me as the image materialized on the screen—a colossal, malignant orb with an inhuman visage at its core. It appeared right over my chest, where the pressure had been released during the cleansing. It was a grotesque reminder of the malevolence that had clung to me like a sinister shadow.

"You see that too, right?" I questioned, making sure I wasn't going batshit crazy.

Joey's fingers became locked around mine. "Mhmmm," he muttered, eyes wide.

All those years, I had questioned my sanity, doubting the validity of the supernatural. But in that chilling moment, I realized the horrifying truth. Something had been attached to me from that old house, an entity that had never truly departed. It had cunningly concealed its malevolence, posing as my old roommate's grandmother to deceive me and gain acceptance.

My life had been a haunting nightmare, a battle against forces that defied comprehension, and I had been an unwitting pawn in a malevolent game played by a denizen of the other side.

Over the coming weeks, I delved deeper into researching the nature of this malevolent entity that seemed to have targeted me. Using what little information the sisters provided, I sought the guidance of paranormal experts and psychics, desperate to find a way to protect myself from its influence. I learned about the importance of shielding and protection rituals and began to practice them diligently.

With time, I regained a sense of control over my life, and my paranormal experiences became less frequent and less unsettling. It was a long and challenging journey, but I had learned to coexist with my sensitivity to the other side while protecting myself from those who meant me harm.

As the years passed, I continued to explore the mysteries of the paranormal, always approaching it with caution and respect. I knew that I would never fully understand the complexities of the spirit world, but I had found a way to navigate it while preserving my own well-being.

The entity that had haunted me for years was gone, but my sensitivity to that side was not. It was a part of me, something that I would always have to deal with whether I wanted to or not. There was no harm in learning how to be a master of both worlds, or so I'd thought.

My experiences had taught me that the line between the living and the dead was not always clear-cut, and that there were forces beyond our comprehension. But I had also learned that with knowledge, respect, and a strong spiritual foundation, I could face the unknown with courage and resilience.

In the end, I had come to accept my sensitivity to the paranormal as a unique part of who I was, and I was determined to use it to help others, guiding them through the mysteries of the unseen world and offering them the protection and support they needed.

I got married years later and carved a life that was finally mine, a sanctuary from the chilling grip of the supernatural. My encounters had evolved into macabre jests, and I was careful to tread cautiously in selecting my interactions. In my home, an old bookcase I thrifted harbored an uninvited but seemingly friendly presence. There were times when it engaged me in playful antics, subtly shifting objects, or orchestrating eerie nighttime taps. Unlike the malevolent attachment of the past, its demeanor remained strangely benign, if not peculiar.

Through time and experience, I'd gained the ability to discern the very essence of each special visitor. When I felt the malicious presence, I addressed the unwelcome with unwavering authority and a cleansing ritual. Which is why I'm not sure how I didn't see this coming.

The last thing I remember from my life was lying in bed, feeling safe.

Thud.

Something fell in the living room. That's okay, it's probably someone passing through, unsure how to interact with the realm in between.

Thud. Thud.

"Did you hear that?" I asked, turning over in bed to rouse my husband.

His breaths were heavy, but he didn't stir.

"Joey. Joey, wake up," I tried again.

He slowly turned toward me, a Cheshire cat grin wide on his face. "I'm awake."

My heart raced, not from the thuds in the living room, but from the unsettling sight before me. This was not the Joey I knew. His eyes were empty, devoid of the warmth and familiarity I had cherished. They were windows to an abyss that sent shivers down my spine.

"What's wrong with you?" I stammered, my voice trembling.

He chuckled, a chilling sound that didn't belong to the man I loved. "Oh, darling, I've been waiting for this moment."

Fear coursed through me, and I tried to scramble out of bed, but my limbs refused to obey. I was trapped, a helpless observer in my own nightmare.

Joey's grin widened further, stretching his lips impossibly wide. It was as if something had taken control of his body, twisting his features into a grotesque caricature.

"You see," he continued, "I've been watching you for a long time, ever since you were just a little girl."

My mind raced, struggling to make sense of the situation. It couldn't be Joey talking. It couldn't be Joey's body that I shared a bed with.

"I knew you had a gift, a connection to the other side. You've always been . . . sensitive to me. Even tried to get rid of me once, so I let you believe that you did. I hung around, hopping from soul to soul in your daily encounters, waiting for the right time," he hissed, the words dripping with malice.

The thuds from the living room grew louder, closer. It was gaining power, feeding off my fear. Understanding dawned upon me, and I couldn't help it as my fear deepened.

As the entity drew closer, my vision filled with darkness. I felt a searing pain, as if something was tearing me apart from the inside. It whispered promises of endless torment and whispered that I would be its prisoner forever.

But just as the darkness threatened to consume me, I felt a surge of strength. The knowledge and wisdom I had gained from years of battling the paranormal surged within me. I fought back, pushing the entity away with all the mental force I could muster.

"In nomine Patris, et Filii, et Spiritus Sancti," I chanted, recalling the words the sisters had used all those years ago. "By the power of the Holy Trinity, I cast you out, foul spirit, from this vessel pure. Release your hold, in God's name, I am sure. Through faith and prayer, your grip shall cease. Return to the darkness, find your release. In nomine Patris, et Filii, et Spiritus Sancti, Amen."

The room seemed to tremble as the entity shrieked in agony. Its hold on Joey faltered, and his eyes returned to normal, filled with confusion and fear.

"Run!" I screamed. "Get out of here!"

Joey needed no further encouragement. He stumbled out of bed and fled the room, leaving me alone in the dark. That wasn't the end of it—I knew that. I'd only bought Joey time.

I'd like to say that's where I can leave things, sign off. That simply isn't true. Take my story as a warning. If you can hear me, then I know you're like me too. You can hear the other side. Maybe you can even see me now. I have unfinished business in this realm, and that's warning you.

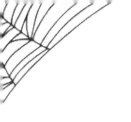

About the Author

Nelle Nikole was born in Corona, California, spent time in the battlefields of Virginia, and now lives in Atlanta with her fiancé, Ben, and their furkid, Sophie. A lifelong reader, she began writing thrilling stories to share with her classmates as early as elementary school. Having lived a little bit of everywhere, Nelle took her studies internationally and completed her anthropology degree by researching abroad in Rio de Janeiro and throughout Cuba. Driven by an insatiable appetite for knowledge, Nelle pursued a Master of Arts in Public Policy, specializing in Global Affairs. Never one to know downtime, Nelle then pursued her lifelong goal of becoming a published author where she is inspired by all things fantasy, apocalyptic and anything in between.

Rising, her sci-fantasy/post-apocalyptic debut novel, speaks to the soul while tackling grief, hope in humanity, and the consequences of betrayal. She uses her real-life experience of living among a variety of lifestyles, cultures, and her overactive imagination to blur the lines of reality and fantasy. In Nelle's debut, a magical, dystopian United States is seen through the eyes of a powerful female main character and her chosen family.

Want more from Nelle Nikole? Give her a follow on social media or purchase book one in her State of the Union trilogy.

Always the Bride

Never the Bridesmaid

Maile Starr

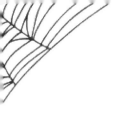

Content/trigger warnings:

Narcissistic behavior, coercive control,
domestic/emotional abuse

LAMMAS

The process of putting on my wedding dress is second nature now. Thin lace straps drape over my shoulders. I pull the corseted back closed myself, then tuck the extra cord underneath the fluffy chiffon skirt. The skirt always needs to be tossed into place and allowed to fall into its naturally large pleats. I do all this myself.

In years past, I had many attendants, all from my coven. Juniper would pull the corseted back closed. Nyx had fluffed and fussed with the skirt. And my mother—my mother, Lenora, head witch of our coven, she had performed all the pre-wedding rituals. She enchanted charms for good health and happiness, cast spells to ward off bad luck, and wove special plants through the strings of my corset.

They've all abandoned me.

It started with Nyx after the second year, then Juniper after the fourth year. This is the first year without my mother. The sixth year. Our sixth anniversary.

I try not to let it bother me too much. So long as we have each other, we'll be alright. All I need is him. All he needs is me.

Anton is incredibly romantic. I've always thought so, but when he promised in his wedding vows that we would renew our vows every year, I just about melted.

He stands at the end of the aisle, the way he's stood every year. He's dressed in a well-fitted black suit with a red tie, smiling at me like I'm the only important person in the world.

His clothing matches our flowers. Blood-red roses and black hollyhocks weave through the wooden awning above us, meticulously laid out the exact way they were on our original wedding day six years ago. Every year at twilight, we escape the modern world and come to our secluded clearing in the woods just before the seasons change. Today, the leaves cling to their trees. Soon, they will change colors and fall to the ground I'm now walking on.

I meet him at the end of the aisle, allowing my fingers to briefly trail through his blond waves before he guides me gently to hold his other hand. He produces a black ribbon, the smell of sweet and tart berries filling the air.

The leader of a coven, my mother, traditionally performs all handfasting ceremonies. Anton insisted on doing it himself from day one. He's incredibly accepting, sometimes even in awe, of my witchy habits. However, having those spells performed on him is out of the question, no matter how much he once trusted my mother—before she abandoned me.

I smile down at our hands. After everything we've been through, it's just the two of us, as it was always meant to be. Anton drapes the black silk over our hands and begins weaving it through our fingers, slowly stitching us together. When our fingers meet, the ribbon is so tight it's almost unbearable.

"Look at me, Calia." He tips my chin up toward him, searching my eyes. "What troubles you?"

"Nothing." I shake my head, forcing a tight smile onto my lips.

He quirks one thick eyebrow at me. "Calia."

"I miss my coven." The words tumble out of me. "A witch is nothing without her coven."

"I know you wish they would be here." His voice is soft and gentle as he lays a comforting hand on my shoulder. "They never should have abandoned you. And I'm sorry that they did." A chaste kiss brushes against my forehead. "I promise I will never leave you, Calia."

I nod, pressing my lips together to stall the tears. My vows fall effortlessly from my lips, and his follow soon after. Our hands make the last turn of the ribbon together. I press my lips to his, relishing the feeling—like warm honey down my throat, coating my sorrows in sweetness. With that, it's done. Another year pledged.

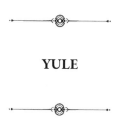

YULE

It's eight months until our next vow renewal. Anton has a late night at the office, as always, and I'm home measuring herbs into my cauldron.

I don't do many spells anymore since most of them require my coven to be nearby. Cooking is a special exception. Anton can stomach uncharmed food—he grew up with it. Only an eighth of the population comes from witching families. I have to have charmed food. Everything else tastes bland to my palate. I can't make myself swallow uncharmed food, so I make two versions of every meal. I don't mind.

I wipe off the remnants of the sauce for Anton's meal on my jeans and turn back toward mine. While I'm measuring out the requisite amount of sage, a puff of deep green smoke emerges from the cauldron. The smoke spills over and coats the floor. A woman's face waits in shadow. I'd know her anywhere, even if I don't have a clear view of her face yet.

I recognize the crooked silhouette of her nose, the signature curve of her curly hairline. Her hair is much longer than it was the last time I saw her, almost down to her waist. Even the large moon earrings that forever hang from her earlobes make themselves known in shadow.

Juniper.

Sage falls from my grasp and lands into the bowl with a fizz. My eyes land on her and refuse to stray. The last time I heard from her, Anton and I had only been married for four years. She'd called me a ditsy bitch who didn't have her head screwed on properly.

It requires a vote to cast someone out of the coven. It was unanimous. They cast me out. And I still don't know why. I can't fathom it. Others have married non-witches, and no one bat an eye. Anton told me I should stop answering her calls because it always made me upset.

I let the cloud of smoke fade away.

Before I can add the next ingredient, the cloud of smoke returns. Juniper is calling again. I let it fade for a second time. Then it crops up a third time. With a resigned sigh, I wave my hand through the smoke. Her face becomes clear, the ruddiness of her cheeks, the light brown wisps of her hair, the deep purple of her eyes.

"Juniper." I cross my arms. "What an honor."

"Calia?" A barely restrained grin creeps across her face. "I'm so glad you picked up! I have wonderful news."

"Oh?"

"Yes! Nyx proposed!"

I blink heavily. "To whom?"

"Me dummy, who else?"

The word slaps me across the face. Dummy. Ditsy.

"Since when have you two been together?"

"Years." She furrows her eyebrows. "We talked about this."

"No, we did not." My arms knit even tighter together. "When would we have talked? Four years ago?" She opens her mouth to respond. "Why haven't you called?"

"What are you talking about?" Juniper's purple eyes start to glow. I take a step back from the cauldron.

I know enough to know when a witch is about to use a spell. "You know perfectly well what I'm talking about."

"No." She takes a step forward, her projected form becoming clearer to me. The caramel tone of her skin appears sickly in contrast with the green smoke. "I really don't. Are you feeling alright?"

"Don't play games with me," I snarl, making to swipe my hand through the smoke. I pause. "Congratulations on your engagement." My hand passes through the bright green smoke, ending the call.

The following week, around the same time, the cauldron emits green smoke again.

Begrudgingly, I answer it. "What?"

"We talked last night."

"No," I insist. "Last night was a Monday, and I was out on a moon-walk."

"You still do those? Those are for children."

"Well, I can't do much else alone, can I?"

She grits her teeth. "We spoke last night. I talked to you. You told me about your day and—"

"Stop trying to convince me you've been calling me, Juniper. You haven't. It's ok, I don't want to deal with your BS, anyway."

"Calia!"

"Goodbye."

Only a few days pass this time before she tries to call again. I don't answer. I don't answer for three days.

And then there's a knock at the front door.

With a flick of my hand, cleaning supplies whirl around the house. Cleaning magic hasn't touched this house in years. Anton's voice rings through the back of my mind, "Cleaning magic is lazy. It doesn't get the job done right. There's nothing that can replace human hands."

I can't help but feel that he's right. In the full thirty seconds I take to get to the door, I'm not fully concentrating on it. Not all the dishes make it into the dishwasher. The broom isn't putting all the dust piles in the same spot. And I don't even have time to inspect the bathrooms. By the time I get to the door, they've done as good a job as they're able, and I send them back to their respective cupboards.

My hand twists behind my head, coaxing my black hair to put itself into a neat, frizz-free bun. My other hand circles around the doorknob and twists it open.

Juniper and Nyx stand on the doorstep, looking deadly serious.

Juniper is wearing dark jeans and a midnight-blue sweater. The only part where her witch shows outwardly is through the multitude of piercings up and down her ears.

Nyx looks nothing like her name would suggest. Her skin is alabaster white, her hair a platinum blond with streaks of strawberry. Even her eyes are the palest shade of blue to exist in humans. Or witches, for that matter. She fills out the slim-fitting, maroon dress she wears nicely, and her fingers are tattooed with runes. It makes it all that much easier for her to cast at a moment's notice.

"What are you doing?" I hold the door halfway closed. They haven't changed a bit since I last saw them.

Juniper and Nyx shoulder past me into the house.

"Cast something." Nyx crosses her arms, squinting at me.

"Why?" I furrow my eyebrows. "You're not being very polite."

"Damn politeness, Calia, cast something," Juniper insists.

I sigh and flick my fingers through the air. Nyx's eyes turn crimson. I fix my gaze on Juniper pointedly. She examines my handiwork and then nods, seemingly satisfied.

"Someone's impersonating you," Juniper says.

"I'll admit, I've never seen you go this far for a lie before. It's ok, you can just admit that you hardly ever called until recently." I cross my arms.

"I'm not lying! Something is wrong."

I roll my eyes. "Who would be—"

The door opens behind them. I close my eyes, steeling myself. Anton steps in wearing a blue button-up shirt and tie, his blond waves slightly messier than they were this morning. I rush forward and give him a quick peck on the cheek, whispering, "I'm sorry. I didn't know they were coming either."

"Ah." He nods stiffly. "Juniper. Nyx. Nice of you to drop by."

Juniper smiles at him, but Nyx is far less enthused.

"Why don't you go take a shower, and I'll have dinner ready for us when you get back down?" That should give him time to adjust to guests. He hates surprises like this.

"Nah." He tosses an arm around my shoulders. "I'll take one later. What brings you two over?"

"Someone's impersonating Calia."

"What are you talking about?" Anton asks. I shoot him a look and roll my eyes. He grimaces.

"For the past few years, I've called you at least once a month on Mondays. And now, suddenly, you don't remember. So either someone has been impersonating you. Or someone made you forget."

"Every month?" I furrow my brows. "Why would you do that?"

"Because I missed you, dummy."

Part of me wants to shoot back that I haven't missed her. But now is not the time for lies. "And you're sure you've been calling this cauldron every time?"

"Yes. It's the same one I called the last two times I called you during the day."

The timer for the oven dings from the kitchen. "Oh!" I exclaim. "Anton, that's your dinner. I'll go—"

"Let's all go," he says. "They're our guests, after all, we should feed them."

Juniper spends the entire time I'm cooking going through lists of rival covens. "There's Nyx's sister's coven!" she exclaims. "Maybe—"

"What reason would she have to impersonate Calia?" Nyx interjects. "I know you don't like her, but it's not her. Trust me."

"Only a witch would be able to answer the call, right?" Anton asks. We nod. "What other witches besides you have access to the cauldron?"

"No one." I shake my head.

Throughout dinner, we swap half-hearted theories back and forth until the sun goes down. Whoever it is obviously doesn't hold any ill will toward us since they have learned nothing of monumental secrecy from our—their—coven. So, we move on to more celebratory topics.

"I heard about your engagement," Anton says. "Congratulations!"

"Thank you." Juniper smiles graciously. "I did have a question for you, though, Calia." She leans forward. "On the other side of my family, the non-witch side, we have a tradition called bridesmaids. It's like a coven's job but—"

"I'm familiar," I interrupt. "Anton told me."

"Oh, great!" She glances at Nyx for confirmation. Nyx nods. "Would you be one of my bridesmaids?"

"Oh." I share a glance with Anton. The girl who called me a ditsy bitch, who voted to have me kicked out of the coven, now wants me to be her bridesmaid? "When is the wedding?"

"August 1st," she continues hurriedly. "In the morning. I know—"

"That's our anniversary," Anton says.

"I know. My mom has an important surgery, so we had to squeeze it in beforehand, just in case. And the venue we wanted only had that day left before it. I'm really sorry I just—" There's a long pause at the table. Her purple eyes flit between me and Anton. "I'd still like you to be my bridesmaid."

"We renew our vows every year on our anniversary." Anton grits his teeth. "She won't be able to. Not on that day."

"But we scheduled it for the morning so that you could still—"

"We spend the whole day preparing," he continues, his jaw tight. "It isn't going to work."

"Ok, then maybe you can do your vow renewals the next day. Just this once." Nyx fixes a cool gaze on him.

I flinch. Anton is practically boiling over with rage. I can't blame him. I am too. They don't speak to me for years, kick me out of the coven, and now they want me to be a bridesmaid on our anniversary?

"Why do you even want me to be your bridesmaid?" My voice is ice. "You both voted me out of the coven yourself. Why do you—"

"Calia, what—"

"You two need to leave," Anton interrupts. "Now. You've insulted my wife one too many times, and I won't stand for it. Leave."

"Insulted?" Nyx's voice is affronted. "What do you—"

"I think you should leave." I stand. "Both of you. Now."

Juniper starts to protest, but Nyx touches her arm briefly. They leave, the door shutting behind them.

He lets out a long breath. I reach out to put a hand on his shoulder. "I—"

"Calia. Never do that again." Anton leans against the door, bolting it shut tight.

"I'm sorry. I didn't know they were coming."

"Next time, don't let them in, okay?"

"I really am sorry, Anton."

"It's fine." He kisses my forehead. "Completely fine. I'll just have to miss my appointment tomorrow to catch up on sleep. Don't worry about it."

I open my mouth to speak again, but he's already halfway up the stairs for bed.

OSTARA

We put my cauldron in the shed after that night. Juniper wouldn't stop calling, and it got too taxing to ignore the green fog that kept spilling over into the living room.

This means that I'm getting used to uncharmed food, but it's a small price to pay for peace. Anton's been thinking about moving sometime soon. Initially, I didn't want to. The roots I have here felt too deep to leave.

Then I realized that all the roots are rotten.

Nyx gone. Juniper, lying to me. And my mother...

What kind of coven abandons one of their own? What kind of mother abandons her daughter? I'm starting to wonder if I'll ever know what it is that I did to them.

Maybe a fresh start will do us some good. He's all I need.

The days creep by, and we get closer and closer to our anniversary...

And Juniper and Nyx's wedding.

LITHA

S omething is pulling me toward the shed, calling from deep within my heart. My cauldron whispers to me—longs for my touch. I long to use it. To answer the call, but I don't dare ask for the key. Colored smoke rises through the shed roof day and night. Sometimes, green smoke. Sometimes, pale blue.

Anton is still at work. I'm cooking dinner, watching the sun cast bright orange rays across the fields.

Black smoke explodes from the shed with such force that it's seeping through the windows and into the house.

The smoke fills my lungs before I can find anything to fight back against it. Every color is too sharp, everything too detailed. My head pounds in rhythm with my heartbeat, and my breaths come in shallow gasps. It's all too much, and I curl up in a ball on the floor with my eyes closed. The world fades away, and I know nothing more.

A nton's arms are around me, shaking me roughly. "Calia." His voice trembles. "What happened?"

I breathe in, the smoky scent of the black smoke entering my lungs once more. My gaze sharpens again. The sun is down now. Anton's wearing his shirt and tie, appearing as though he had just returned from work. What is it that he does again?

I take in another shaky gasp, the black smoke circling around my lips. A thought comes to me clear as day. "I want to be Juniper's bridesmaid."

"I—what?" He blinks. "No. I meant with the smoke. And you passed out on the floor."

"I want to be Juniper's bridesmaid. That's what I want." My voice comes out as croaky as a toad's.

He surveys the smoke around us, then scoops me into his arms. I'm vaguely aware of the door opening and the cool night air on my face. He opens the car door, depositing me in the passenger seat. I stay there, whispering for Juniper.

He returns and sits in the driver's seat beside me, spoon feeding me soup. It's delicious and fragrant. Colors return to normal. The world becomes less sharp. The black smoke is gone. "What do you want now?" he asks. "Do you still want to be Juniper's bridesmaid?"

"No," I croak with smoke coated lungs. "I want to be with you."

"That's what I thought." He pulls me into his arms. "She's trying to put a spell on you. We have to get rid of the cauldron." I nod even as my heart calls out for it.

LAMMAS

The morning of our anniversary, the morning of Juniper's wedding, Anton is away setting up for our seventh vow renewal. I curl up on the couch and eat the special breakfast he prepared for me. The smell of the rose and hollyhock syrup that he made is intoxicating. I pour some of it over spiced oats.

This is the only uncharmed food that I love without reserve. Some of it comes from witch recipes, some from his own home, creating the perfect marriage of flavors—the perfect matching of souls.

There's a knock on the door. I approach wearily, but by the time I open the door, whoever it was is long gone. All that remains is a large, white box.

When I open the box, a puff of black smoke spills out. Everything comes into sharp focus. I wave my hand through the air to mitigate some of the worst effects.

My fingers wrap around something soft and slippery. I pull it out of the box. A gorgeous dress of sage-green silk tumbles down to the floor in ripples. Spaghetti straps hold it up, the neckline pooling around where the collarbone would be. It has a tasteful slit and an open back.

I think I might like it even better than my wedding dress. I haven't worn a formal gown other than my wedding dress in years. A note falls from the folds of the dress. I bend down to pick it up, wondering if it's a note from Anton.

Calia,

I know that today is really important for you. But it's really important for me too. It doesn't feel right without you here. If you change your mind, the offer still stands. Will you be my bridesmaid?

I stare at the dress. Juniper sent this to me. Juniper bought this for me. She still remembers my dress size and everything.

I check the back of the note and find details about the wedding, including the address, the time, and where to meet them. My wedding dress is already laid out across the chair.

I look between my wedding dress and the sage dress. Which to wear?

I can't. I can't go. Anton would be crushed. I lay the dress down on the couch reluctantly. It really is gorgeous. A small puff of black smoke escapes the folds of the dress. I inhale it before I can think about holding my breath.

Minutes later, I'm out the door, doing my hair up on the way to the bus. I hope I'm not too late.

I take the stairs up to the bridal suite two at a time, but just outside the door, I stop.

Why am I here? Why am I wearing this dress? Today's my anniversary. I should be wearing my wedding dress.

Another bridesmaid wearing a matching dress opens the door. Behind her, Juniper stands in front of a mirror. She's wearing a slim fitting gown of white silk with an open back that displays her moon phase tattoos crawling up her spine. Her hair is pinned up in a roll.

"Calia!" She tackles me in a giant hug. "I didn't think you would come."

"I wouldn't miss this for the world."

Black smoke hangs around my head. It's getting harder and harder to remember what could have possibly been more important than this. Anton is doing something today, but for the life of me I can't think what.

Their wedding is an intimate and small affair. Juniper and Nyx walk themselves down the aisle from opposite ends, meeting in the middle.

A woman stands in the center, a sage-green ribbon held between her bony fingers. Her black curls are pulled into a voluminous bouffant from which sprigs of sage sprout. A black dress glides over her curves, tied around the middle with a belt of stars. Bright white eyes peer out of hooded eyelids. It's a long moment before I recognize her as my mother.

She smiles at me, but her focus is on our coven's happy couple. The handfasting ceremony wraps their hands together rather than stitching them as closely and tightly as they will go. My mother whispers her incantations over them—charms for a happy and long life together.

Halfway through their first dance, my mother stands beside me. She doesn't say a word. She just reaches out for my hand. I latch on as tightly as I can, barely catching the tears before they slide down my cheeks.

The reception is in full swing. The sun is only just beginning to set. I step out for a moment to catch my breath, to take in the night. I haven't had a night out since I can't remember when. I haven't danced in so long. I haven't seen my mother in so long.

"What are you doing?" a man's voice hisses.

I spin on the spot, and there is Anton, blond waves in disarray. I furrow my eyebrows at him. "I'm her bridesmaid."

"I came home to get you, and I didn't know where you were! I was so worried. You're lucky I found the card. How could you do this to me? We promised each other!"

"Do what?" Something has been nagging at me all day, I just have no idea what it is.

"We renew our vows tonight, Calia. You told Juniper no. I—" He furrows his brows and waves his hand in front of my face. I watch as the cloud of black smoke dissipates. "She's been cursing you to do what she wants, don't you see?"

I do see. She made me forget what was important about today. I can't believe I didn't see it. "Oh Anton, I'm so sorry. I didn't—"

He clasps my face in his hands. "It's alright. Let's go. Let's get away from her. We need to move. I've been telling you this."

The sun is setting. We need to renew our vows soon, or it will be too late for twilight. He secures me in the passenger seat, then drives off toward our venue, our little spot in the middle of the woods.

The process of putting on my wedding dress has become second nature. Only, my fingers won't do it. They know the routine, but I can't make myself put the wedding dress on.

Something is wrong, but I don't know what.

Eventually, Anton takes pity on me and helps me into the dress. He walks me down the aisle himself, black ribbon in hand.

Deep red roses and black hollyhocks line the archway in the same intricate pattern as always. Candles are lit in a circle around us. I never noticed the candles before today. Before, I had eyes only for him at the end of the aisle.

I don't give him my hand, but he takes it anyway.

When I turn to look at him, I don't see Anton. Not the Anton I know. His brows are furrowed in rage, every vein in his neck is sticking out. His muscles are so tense that the mere feeling of his fingers on me hurts. He looks positively monstrous.

Juniper upset him greatly. I can understand why. I wouldn't want someone bewitching and taking control over him either.

"Hey." I take his face in my hand. "It's alright. I'm here. And tomorrow, we'll get far away from her."

He nods shortly, the ghost of a smile passing over his face. His fingers weave through mine and the black ribbon follows, the intoxicating smell of berries perfuming the air. The ribbon digs deep into my skin, deeper than usual. I don't say anything. I don't want to ruin the moment.

A cloud of black envelopes us. I freeze where I stand. Everything comes into sharp focus around me—the flowers, the candles, the ribbon, Anton himself.

He looks around frantically for the source. It doesn't take me long to find it. I follow the smoke trail to the end of the clearing. Juniper stands in her white dress, smoke issuing from her fingertips. "He doesn't love you!" she shouts.

I look back at him, my eyes sharp and my ears attuned. I never realized just how dulled my senses had been. He's ugly. Not because of his appearance, but the expression he wears on his face—malice and hatred.

"This is a spell, Calia," Juniper calls.

"THIS is a spell?!" Anton yells. "You have smoke coming from your hands." He waves a hand in front of my face. There's a break in the smoke.

He isn't ugly at all. He's so handsome, so gentle. I love him.

Black smoke clears my vision again, and he looks monstrous. I lean away from him.

The ribbon between us snaps. I tumble backward, only now realizing that the only thing holding me up was Anton. My eyes find him on the ground, holding one half of the ribbon in his hand.

Nyx holds a sharp knife in one hand and my half of the ribbon in the other. "Look around Calia," she implores.

"Doesn't it look familiar?" Juniper asks.

The candles are all in a circle around us. The altar directly at the center. The flowers in the trellis, the hollyhocks forming runes.

I do remember this. I remember this from long, long ago when my mother first taught me rune magic. For a bewitching spell to work, you needed three things. You needed candles. You needed the flowers specific to your needs—fertility and romance in this case. And, most importantly, you needed visible runes.

I meet Anton's eyes. The black ribbon's putrid, intoxicating smell wafts through the air. It's coated in a potion. A potion made from roses and hollyhocks. A potion that, up until moments ago, was seeping into my skin.

"No." I shake my head. "You wouldn't. I love you. I—" God, do I love him? With this black smoke around me, I'm not sure I do. Weren't we on the verge of breaking up at the end of our first year of marriage?

"Calia," Juniper says. "We never voted you out of our coven. It's him who's been pretending to be you. He's filled your head with lies."

"Calia," he beckons, his voice soft. "I told you she didn't want us together. I told you she was jealous. Look." I hesitate, peering up at Juniper, the vitriol in her eyes. "Calia, there's still time. Come here."

I stand. I want to. I love him. I'm his. All I need is—"NO."

He splutters, making his way to his feet. "COME HERE, CALIA!"

Something in his voice compels me to obey, despite the black smoke hanging in the air.

Because I love him. I love him. I love him. I—

"Calia," a soft voice breaks through the fog.

I whip around. "Mother?"

She stands behind me, dousing candles with a flick of her wrist. "It's true. He's been doing this for years. We didn't think he knew rune magic. We thought he was like the rest of the humans, and he flew right under the radar. I thought that all of these," she gestures at the runes, "were his attempt at respecting your upbringing. I didn't recognize the signs, and I'm sorry."

"But," I look at Anton, the way he glares at my mother with hatred in his eyes, "he doesn't come from a witch family, he couldn't have done—"

"I did some digging," Nyx supplies. "His great-grandmother abandoned her coven. The whole family has been pretending to be human for generations."

"We thought you hated us. That you'd renounced witchcraft for him," my mother says.

"But when someone else was speaking to me as you every month," Juniper starts to explain.

"And when he freaked out at the mere thought of moving a vow renewal by one day." Nyx steps between me and Anton, brandishing the knife at him.

"We knew," mother finishes. "Tonight is when the spell is weakest—when it has to be renewed. It had to be tonight."

Anton's eyes plead with me. I stare back, but my gaze flickers away from him. And in that moment, he jumps.

Nyx and Anton scuffle in front of me, the silver of the knife glinting in the night air. Juniper cries out, but she doesn't stop performing what I now recognize as a counter-curse. Black smoke fills the air around me. Mother sends a gust of wind toward them, toppling Anton over, but also Nyx. The knife skitters away across the dirt and grass.

I dive for it before anyone else can grab it and scramble on top of Anton, pinning him down with my weight. "Calia," he whispers frantically. "I told you, didn't I? I told you that your coven was messed up. Look at them. Look at what they're doing to us."

I raise the knife above my head, preparing to plunge it downward. Is this what I want?

"Calia, please," he whimpers. "Put it down. You don't know what you're doing." I stay frozen, poised to strike, but unable to do it. "You love me. You don't want to do this." I don't move. "Juniper is lying to you. I don't need a spell to keep you around. You love me."

That face. I love that face. I love him. I love Anton. I can't do this to him. I can't do this. Do I want to do this? Do I really?

"Do you love me?" The words spill unwillingly from my mouth.

"Of course, I do."

"What do you love about me, Anton?"

"I love how beautiful you are. I love the way you dress. I love the meals you cook and the way the house smells when I come home from work. I love you. You are everything I want."

I lean forward, letting the knife fall to my side. "You love me?"

"Yes. Please, Calia, see reason."

His eyes are wet and wide with fear. I throw my arms around him. "I'm so sorry I scared you, Anton. I'm sorry. Are you alright?"

He wraps one arm around me as tightly as he can. "Yes, darling. I'm alright."

"You promise?" I press a desperate kiss to his lips. "You promise you'll be alright?"

"Yes. I promise. Let's just go home alright?" I nod, burying my face into his shoulder. He turns to Juniper and my mother. "You're going to stay away from us." They take several steps forward. He throws out a hand toward them. The candles around us flicker back on, then off again. "You're going to stay away, or there will be consequences."

My mother flexes her fingers in a fury. An invisible spell barrels toward us. I throw a hand up to block it, drawing from the power of my coven being near again. A wall made of air surrounds Anton and I, protecting us.

"I'm going to love you forever," I whisper to him. I pick up the severed pieces of ribbon and drape one half over my wrist and the other over his.

He beams at me, sweeping me into his embrace. A silent argument passes between him and my mother, a challenge. He turns from her and leads me away from my coven.

Or at least, what he thinks is me. I will leave my imprint on him. I watch Anton leave with my projection, a picture-perfect image of what he wanted me to be.

With a heavy sigh, I release the magic, still on my knees on the ground next to the altar.

"You love what I can do for you," I whisper, allowing my hands to fall to my sides. The version of me that loved Anton slowly fades from existence.

Juniper kneels beside me, her voice soft. "You had the knife. Why didn't you—"

"Because he kept me under a spell for seven years. I'm going to return the favor."

"What did you do?" Nyx places a hand on Juniper's shoulder.

"I used the remnants of his magic on him. It's the same spell, he just thinks that he's still married to me. That I'm going home with him. That I'm going to cook him dinner and have his children and labor away over a stove and never use my magic again."

Mother is the last to join me. She picks up the knife gingerly, kneeling in front of me. I rotate on the spot to face her, palm held out. She makes a tiny shallow cut across my love line, cleansing it and renewing it, then pulls me into her arms.

"Welcome back, Calia."

About the Author

Maile Starr writes stories laced with sarcasm, graveyards, and magic. She's published several short stories around the internet and is absolutely thrilled to be a part of this anthology!

By day (and night), Maile is a bartender. By even later night, she writes her upcoming debut novel *The Marbhaven Reaper*. She lives in Colorado with her husband and is obsessed with bay windows. She'll know she's made it when she has a bay window reading nook. Maile loves hearing from readers. Go check out her website to stay in touch!

———◈———

https://mailestarr.wixsite.com/linesinthestarrs
https://www.instagram.com/linesinthestarrs/

Beacon

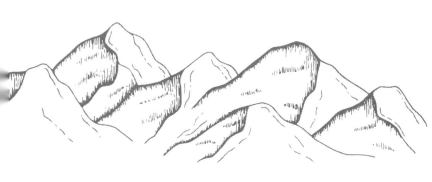

Kelly Virens

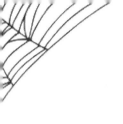

Content/trigger warnings:

Death, injury description, memories of witnessing
a murder (magic induced, not gory)

The weather was still warm. This time of the year always brought warm nights and even warmer days. Rain fell elsewhere these months, leaving the air dry and the soil dusty. It was a wonder that the sugar pines and the firs remained true to their name as evergreens. The blooms and other trees certainly were withered and dormant.

The moon was making a dramatic entrance on the horizon as the sun bid a farewell glow over it. The peaks of the mountains loomed over the town, casting a cascading veil of shadow. Despite the heat, snow from the long, wet winter remained, creating patches of blinding, white emptiness under the day's sun. The snow patches yielded a shimmer against the sky full of gradients, the orange shifting to a black canvas full of pinholes.

Harper walked into the tavern, relaxed but still alert. She had traveled most of the day and finally cleaned up. She embraced feeling refreshed from her shower after a day of hiking. The aroma of poultry and rice made her mouth water, and a chilled mead was just what she needed. Tales were told by the many patrons in the tavern, while others were deep in various card games. She watched two men playing openly with their daggers, noting they both had a certain flair of arrogance. She was grateful when her food arrived, as she did not want to make eye contact with any of the patrons.

Harper Gaffney had little time to entertain the idea of friends and even less time for would-be foes. For the Gaffney line rested on her now. The estate had been lost, her family had perished, and the land was in decay. There was little to save aside from a name that was as good as cursed for all she knew. She hadn't wanted the family business—it too was tarnished. Running was all that Harper Gaffney could do.

The meal hit the spot. So much so that Harper stared at the bowl for a moment with a satisfied smile on her face. As she finished her mead, her ears focused once again on the tales floating around the tavern. She was a ranger, tried and true. Traveling north from Kentridge, she had never left the safety of the southern territory. Having studied at a prestigious ranger academy there, she learned all she could about tracking, weapons, and reading the land. She wasn't a distinguished ranger yet—she did not bear the mark—and she was fine with that. Especially given the territory she was in. The king of Renton had a chokehold on most of the continent, and he was deplorable. She wanted little to do with the history of this place. What she wanted was a fresh start. Harper wanted to forget the name Gaffney entirely.

She let her ears listen to more of the surrounding conversations homing in on one in particular.

"The innkeeper runs a medical practice on the side. The king exiled him," an older man said. His voice was rusty.

"Ahh, his cousin was the dead queen," another voice chimed in. This one a little smoother than the first.

"Aye. He is seeking the moon lotus flower. He will pay a hefty bounty for it."

She listened to them talk, but her thoughts ran wild with possibilities of a bounty. The plant was highly desired for its medicinal uses. Every part was used for a salve, tea, elixir, or medicine in some fashion or another. It was a rare flower to find, and for an exiled doctor-turned-innkeeper, it would be dangerous. For a ranger though, especially one with her gifts, it would be easy.

She thought of all she could do with that bounty. If she got just one plant, she would be set for a while. Two would secure a future for her. The excitement had long since overridden the satisfaction of her meal and shower.

Harper stood up and walked over to the two talking.

"What does this flower look like, and where is it?" Harper asked, watching the two assess her, their eyes fixed on her weapons.

The older one smirked and eyed the other. "That is a lot of weapons for a little girl," he laughed.

"Ranger's need weapons," Harper snapped out. "Tell me about the flower."

The two bellowed a laugh as she rolled her eyes.

"Brave little ranger, where this flower is, your weapons are of no use. Your weapons are designed for hunting prey. You will soon find that the dead prey upon you."

Harper sighed. "Let me guess, no one knows what the flower looks like? It's only seen once every five hundred years, and only the purest of hearts can pull it free from the earth." Sarcasm rippled through her words. The two let out another hearty laugh.

"Ahh, you may be a ranger, but you're still a child waiting for a bedtime story where even the most broken hearts can be saved by a hero," the older man replied.

"Just tell me what it looks like and where to find it. I don't have time for fairy tales and heroes that are only interested in damsels."

"Well, the moon lotus looks as you'd expect—a white lotus with a yellow center. However, they are only visible under moonlight when it illuminates, hence the name. Sure, there are white flowers in the Valley of Lost Souls, but these ones can only be seen at night, under a cloudless sky. Much like tonight."

"And the Valley of Lost Souls is where?" she asked.

"North of here. It is connected to the Starlit Woods, directly in the shadow of Lassen Peak. Some folks do not realize they have wandered into the valley, though, as it is identical to the rest of the woods. In the daytime, it is generally safe. At night, however, is when it becomes a hunting ground. The cedars, firs, and sugar pines are plenty, but other trees grow in the valley, too—species not usually found here and not native to the area. Odd place it is," the man with the smoother voice explained.

"I'm not worried about beasts that prowl the forests or mismatched trees." Harper's patience was diminishing. "I will get that flower to the innkeeper and get my reward. Thank you for the information. Enjoy your ales and tales." She turned to take a step.

"Be careful, little ranger. The valley is ruled by a forest king, who enjoys collecting souls. The flowers are said to be beacons to lure souls in. A moth to a bright light. Rumor has it when you touch the flower, he claims your soul. So do not touch it with your skin. Use gloves or something," the rougher voice spoke.

Harper turned back and scowled at them, not buying it. From what she had heard, the king of Renton was a tyrant and certainly did not want anyone encroaching on his territory. Not to mention, everything from Kentridge's border to beyond Lassen Peak, including the western to eastern coasts, was Renton's rule. Two kings? No map had ever shown another kingdom within Renton's territory. She shook her head and took another step.

"The King of Lost Souls is particularly fond of witches. It is said he enjoys collecting them, all types, and his collection is not complete, either. If you have any witch's blood in you, it'd be best not to seek that flower."

Stopping her stride toward the exit, she stared at the floor and pushed an audible gust of air through her nose.

"I'm a ranger. I'm not a witch. I don't believe in silly campfire stories."

"Remember, that which is unclaimed cannot be stolen," one said with a tone of warning. Harper stood for a second longer, then walked out of the tavern. Tonight, she would get that reward money. Without a second thought or glance, she went north toward the valley.

Walking through town, she passed by people milling about. Some were drunk, and some were hurrying home. Some had weapons strapped to their backs. Others watched her, checking over their shoulders as though there were ghosts looming in the streets.

An old woman appeared to be asleep on the ground, leaning against a building. Her dirty, tattered clothes and matted hair indicated she had lived a hard life. Some coin could be spared—Harper considered it a good deed. Besides, she would be rich when she got back to the inn.

Harper reached into her pocket and dug out some coins. Not wanting to wake or startle her, she set the coins down on a cloak nearby the woman.

Suddenly, the sound of ocean waves crashing rang in her ears. The ebb and flow of the tide pulsed as though it were her heart. A cold breeze swirled around Harper, and then a voice flowed into her ears. She spun around, quickly pulling out her dagger in one smooth motion.

"Little coastal witch, so far from home. That which is unclaimed cannot be stolen. Little coastal witch." A woman's words lulled together in a soft melody. Harper turned around to see the woman's eyes cloudy and vacant. "The ocean coursing through your veins, how it swells and breaks. What might you be doing in the shadow of Lassen?" The ode seemed to caress Harper's skin, sending a chill down her spine. "Oh, little coastal witch, so far from home."

Harper turned and kept her eyes focused on the road ahead. With each step she took, the tendrils of the chant lingered as if it were a foul stench. That bitter reminder of why she was so far from home. She wanted to bury it, and that was hard to do when everyone in this town was able to sense her magic.

She had no desire to head back to her hometown of Askra Falls. The town could count it as a blessing that the Gaffney line was gone. She would bury it and watch it all but be forgotten.

J ust outside of the town was a town hall with a place for various postings and a map of the area. Harper's eyes roved the trails, and she noted the forks in the trail. This was easy enough for a ranger. She would be there in no time. And she was right.

The path took her through the Starlit Woods, passing a few residences with hearths billowing smoke. The peak of Lassen was obstructed by the denseness of the trees. Once she had navigated the forks on the trail, all she had was a straight shot through until she could see the peak. Then she'd take a left and would be in the Valley of Lost Souls. The shadow from the moonlight was darkest here.

While she had walked, she had heard various animals, some large and some small. Identifying them was easy for even a novice ranger. Small game scampered about, and various fowl scattered between the ground and the trees. The apex predators she ignored while they watched her. Curious beasts, they were—they had never seen this coastal magic.

Something in her stung. A memory that ached as though a thorn snagged her. It was the magic inside her that she loved but had driven Gaffney to crumble. That coastal magic was a muscle doused in atrophy, and yet, even here, it couldn't help but slip out to offer peace of mind to those apex predators. Still, she trudged on, refusing to dwell on it.

Her mind had been distracted and only now registered how dark it had gotten. Sure enough, the peak was right ahead. She was in the shadow of Lassen. More snow clung stubbornly to this side of the mountain. As Harper took in the Valley of Lost Souls, she noticed the different types of trees. There were still the cedars, firs, and sugar pines she expected to see, yet the ones here were all perfectly lined up, as though planted there between nonnative species of trees. One row had a towering coast redwood. Another row had a birch tree, and next to it, not breaking the grid, was a ginkgo tree adjacent to a palm tree. She knew these trees grew in different climates. Lassen's summers were far too hot and dry, the winters far too cold and caked with snow, for many of these trees to grow.

Taking in the sight of all these trees in a grid, she felt a coolness slither through the air. Her eyes were beginning to see things her mind could not process. Every trunk appeared to have an echo of a pulse. Every beat sent ripples through the varying textures of the bark. Shaking her head slowly in disbelief, she walked along the outside of the grid, parallel to the mountain range, to search for the moon lotus.

Moving with quiet, careful steps, she noticed the grid appeared incomplete, as though whoever made this grid was waiting to find more seeds to plant. A yellowwood, a maple, a weeping willow, and a banyan tree were all in this odd assortment of a grid. She stopped examining the trunks—her eyes kept seeing them pulse with a current. She told herself that it was just the shadows playing tricks on her eyes, so she focused on the tops of the trees instead.

A vision of waves came crashing over her. The whitewash knocked her over, sending a tremble through her body. Her senses were overtaken by the scent of the salty sea air and the loud crash-

ing of the waves roaring despite the water plugging her ears. A
gasp for breath, and she remembered trying to push herself up.
Her power soothed the waves, and she crawled to shore when a
woman cried out for her. It was her mom, yet she seemed terrified.

The memory replayed for Harper here, in the shadow of
Lassen. The nearest ocean was a three-day trek by foot. Though
if one could catch a wagon, it'd cut the time in half. Not that
Harper was going near an ocean, not after what had happened.

The blow of a horse's breath sounded from behind with her
next step, and she spun around, drawing her sword. Nothing
was there. She turned in a full circle, ready to swing, but found
nothing. The air was still and silent—no horse, no waves. Then,
as though the earth had held its breath, the crickets began their
nightly chorus again, owls hooted, and small rodents squeaked.
Harper returned her sword to its sheath on her back and pro-
ceeded walking. She veered left into the woods, away from the
grid.

A feeling of eyes on her danced along her skin. It did not
scare or worry her. Harper had been through enough people
watching her every move. If someone was out here, she'd prove
a difficult target.

With every step she took, her eyes scanned for white flowers,
finding nothing. Small, glowing bugs appeared, and at first, she
thought they were fireflies, but it was far too dry in this region
for them. Winters got too cold, blanketing everything in white.
Calls of coyotes echoed alongside the screeching of mountain
lions and pulled her attention in every direction. Yet the further
she walked, no glowing flowers could be seen.

Her steps slowed her to a statue as she came upon a woman kneeling in front of a tree, a basket by her side. The tree was one that was pulsing with life. The woman's honey-blond hair was pulled to the side and braided, forming a crown atop her head. She wore a billowing long-sleeved shirt, cinched at the waist with a black belt. The shirt hung over black fitted pants.

Harper could hear whispers of a chant with a familiar tune, but the words were spoken in a dialect of Shadow's Ridge, which was west of here, on the other continent. Harper knew this, too, from her days at the academy. How prestigious her education was, all for it to be wasted.

This melody the woman sang called to Harper's coastal magic. It was a prayer chant her grandmother had taught her to wish lost souls a safe journey to wherever the great beyond took them. It was a witch's chant. The academy hadn't taught her anything about being a witch—magic use was banned. All the magic that thrummed in her blood was from her grandmother and mom. They had mentioned that similar prayers and chants carried the same tune, but the words could be in a foreign tongue. They were said to be that way so that witches could pay their respects to each other, regardless of where they came from.

Waves crashed in her ears again, but this was not violent like before. It was the current passing under her before the wave broke. The calming weightlessness that she had been missing since she left home. Her eyes caught the woman's body tense, and she turned around. Graceful, but not at all ready to defend. This was not a defensive stance, Harper assessed. This was a shocked, caught-off-guard stance.

Their eyes locked, and Harper felt her jaw gape at her beauty. Her eyes were soft and a blueish green that reminded Harper of the headland's waters back home. She had a narrow frame with skin that appeared soft and lightly sun-kissed as if she had been out here all day under the summer sun. Harper took in her beautiful face and the expression mirroring her own. Surely, this woman wouldn't be as taken aback by Harper's short, black bob haircut and curvy, muscular frame. She knew her outfit of baggy pants with pockets on the side and zip-up sleeveless shirt was likely not flattering, but it was practical.

Harper relaxed her stance. "Hello, sorry if I startled you. What are you doing out here?"

The woman remained shocked.

"This place is dangerous," the woman said. Her voice was like honey upon Harper's ears.

"Should you be here with just a basket? I see no weapons." Harper responded.

"I know these woods. I live here." She paused for a moment as though she were not sure how to continue. "You really should not be here."

"I am fine. I know how to use all of these. Shouldn't you be home? It is dark."

"Which is exactly why you should go. There are things lurking, eyes watching." The woman glanced around nervously.

"There is a job I must do here. You should go if it is not safe."

The woman looked frustrated now. Her eyes traveled up and down Harper's body, and her despair grew. "You are a ranger, but also a witch?" she asked nervously.

"Ranger."

"I am a mountain witch. I sense your magic—it is near feral from disuse. You need to go. Now. I know what you seek, and you cannot continue. Go back to town."

"I need to find it, but I do not wish to see these dangerous things you fear harm you too. Please. Go back home. Was it one of the cottages outside of town?"

The ocean waves crashed loudly, violently again in Harper's ears, slamming the breath out of her. She saw her mother running toward her. 'Go back Harper, let the deity sister protect you, she will keep you safe.' Harper felt a wave drag her back. She saw her mom's face full of terror, and then her dad running toward them from the shore. His face had gone mad with rage. 'Go back!'

A thundering sound shot down into Harper's skull. "Do not move. Hold your breath as long as you can," she heard, but this was not her mom's voice—it was the woman's voice. The woman in the shadow of Lassen. Harper shook her head in confusion. Memories were blurring together with reality. Memories she did not want to have. The thundering noise got louder, and she looked at the woman who had come closer.

"Hold your breath and slow your pounding heart," she said sternly. Harper knew it was sage advice, so she took a deep inhale and tried to calm herself.

In the distance, a herd of elk pounded their hooves on the ground as they ran. Their skulls illuminated under the moonlight as though their skin and fur were shrouded in silk, and yet, the animals seemed very much alive. Harper stared frozen, not believing her eyes as she took in the animals' glowing, white bones showing through their fur.

"Do not move," the woman repeated sternly.

Harper watched an elk far bigger than all the others, with a rider atop its back. The reins glistened as if made of polished silver and onyx stones. Her heart threatened to pound, and a gasp clawed up her throat.

"My name is Layla. I am a mountain witch from Shadow's Ridge." Her voice was hushed but fast.

Harper cut her eyes to her.

"Your magic and mine must have sensed each other despite the—" Layla paused. "The difference between us. I moved here a year ago." The thundering elk passed, and the herd and the rider were out of view. "It is safe now."

A huge exhale escaped Harper's body. "What was that?" Her voice was shaky. Her hand instinctively had gone for her dagger at her hip.

"If you know of the moon lotus, I assume you have heard talk of the forest king."

"That is not real," Harper said. Layla looked unamused.

"Then you mustn't be a ranger nor a witch if you are that blind to your instincts. Your eyes are not deceiving you. Now leave and go back to town where it is safe."

"But what about you?! Are you coming?"

"Eventually. I needn't worry. I live here."

Harper swallowed hard and narrowed her eyes at Layla. "No. I need to get that moon lotus. I'm not leaving until I do."

"You don't need what it brings. What type of witch are you? It's certainly not common here."

"I don't want to talk about it. I need to get this moon lotus so I can move on with my life."

"Do you have a name?"

"Harper."

Layla smiled a bit.

"Walk with me at least a little way? You know what the king is searching for, right?"

Harper nodded and started walking, watching for any of the flowers. She realized how quiet Layla's steps were. Even quieter than her own. The sensation of others nearby tingled her skin as though they were passing by, paying no mind, yet there was nothing save for a cool breeze, a weight floating by she could not see.

"Souls. He cannot steal that which is unclaimed. I belong to no one. My family is gone, and I need to bury all ties to the name."

Layla frowned. "That is not what those words mean, Harper."

The sound of her name in Layla's voice snagged her attention. The gentle sound of waves ebbed and flowed.

"I have seen many come through here in search of the moon lotus. They are beacons for him, though. Those who seek the flower do not leave. I do not wish to see that happen to you. Regardless of what you are running from, it is not worth the risk of being bound here to him and part of his collection," she said. "Please, I do not want to see you fall to that fate."

"I take it he already has a mountain witch from the ridge?" Harper scoffed. Layla dropped her gaze and nodded.

"My mother." Such sorrow coated her words, and Harper knew her pain.

"I'm sorry." Harper wished she'd bite her tongue more. "I lost my mother too, and my father at the same time."

"I would rather not have to sing the chants for you, as well. I come here to where the king laid her to rest in that tree. She saved me from a similar fate that she met. She sacrificed herself for me. We were not aware of the beacons, and yet she was lured in by it and not thinking clearly when he showed up. She told me to run and shoved me and I tripped—fell. Then he took her," Layla explained.

"I'm sorry." Harper repeated the small words that would never offer enough in return.

"If I'd had the chance to run back to town, maybe we could have met. Maybe I would have stayed there. You are beautiful."

Harper blushed. "You are too." Her mind processed Layla's words. "You don't go into town? It is only a short walk. You must need provisions and supplies. It does not appear as though much grows here. Save for the grid of non-native trees somehow."

"They are placed there. Have you seen it?"

"I did. Shortly before I found you."

"The king's collection," Layla scoffed.

"I thought it was souls."

"Yes," Layla said. "Which is why you need to leave."

"The souls are trees? He places them there?"

"They grow into a tree native to the soul's birthplace. The bodies are picked up by the guards. It is said that their king sends the disobedient guards on these sweeps to collect the fallen, the soulless. Very few have figured that out, and even fewer would be able to tell the tales. So, word travels that the moon lotuses are his beacons because they are an extension of his magic. With earth magic in them, the flower offers many medicinal uses, but to remove one is no small feat."

"Yet you know all this, but you don't tell anyone? Why?"

Layla remained quiet, and sad eyes met Harper's, yet no tears formed.

"She saved me the only way she knew how," Layla said with despair. "Please, I cannot bear the thought of seeing that happen again to you. I know we only just met, but you have your whole life ahead of you and a world to explore. A new start you seem to be trying to reach for. Please go."

The waves graced Harper once again, and her eyes fixed on Layla.

"Come with me? Or I can stay in town, and you can come too?"

"No. You can't stay. Please. The tavern has comfortable rooms. They are safe. There are wagons that leave every morning. North, there's a ranger's post there, just beyond Ember Falls. I remember passing it on my way here."

The waves started to get louder. She heard her mother again calling for her, telling her to go back in the water. Her mom pushed her back, the waves pulling her. Her father was enraged. His eyes were not his own.

"Harper! Go back. He mixed the solarium bane with too many other tonics which had an adverse effect. The house. Harper, the house! He slaughtered everyone."

She turned to look at the grand estate now and saw it burning, thick black smoke blocking out the sun. Her father was always striving to gain as much knowledge as he could for his quest to take revenge on the tyrant king for hurting the dead queen. The queen had been studying to be a mage—a pure one, one the earth spoke to. Every day, her father grew more irate at not being able to master the correct combination to amplify his mage abilities. Mages stuck together, always, and the town of Iris glade was a haven for them. The queen had learned there, and her father learned at the mage academy there a decade before.

In the water, she recalled her mom sending out a wave of her coastal magic, encasing Harper in an air bubble and pushing her under.

Harper's screams were caught in the bubble as she watched the flames shoot out of her father's hands and her mother fall. He seethed and ran for Harper, but the sea swallowed her and kept her down.

Such a strong force shot through Harper, that atrophied muscle awakening in her core, the one that started the tidal wave to rid the earth of Gaffney Estate. When she surfaced, she choked and spat out the saltwater as it burned her lungs and nose.

"She's alive! She made it!" a voice called. Hands hoisted her up, and Harper didn't know what was happening—she couldn't feel anything.

The sounds of water splashed, and her feet were wet. Harper gasped and glanced down. It was night, and she was in a forest.

"You're a coastal witch! From Askra Falls? That's—Harper, that is so far away, you have to go! Now!" Layla cried out.

Harper blinked, still staring at her feet. She heard Layla's words, but her body wouldn't move. She was in mud. The dusty soil was now mud. She was unsure if Layla had seen the vision, but Harper knew the scent of saltwater, and the wet ground was evident.

"Harper!" Layla's screams made her look up.

The thundering hooves pounded the earth once more.

"Hold your breath, calm yourself!" Layla pleaded. "Please let's go! Follow me. I will get you out of here."

Harper's eyes took in the trail Layla was blocking. It was down a cliffside and easy to navigate even in the dark. Her eyes followed it right to a moon lotus. Her heart pounded harder—as hard as the hooves against the earth.

"Harper don't. Please."

She met Layla's frantic eyes. Harper wondered why Layla was not more scared or crying. Her eyes appeared as though they would have tears. Once again, she found herself turning her gaze to the moon lotus.

"Wait!" Layla called out for her. The wispy, pale hand reached for her, but she pulled it away. Harper's eyes registered this as she studied the woman. "That's not the way."

"I see one, though. I see the flower, and he's nowhere nearby. I have to get this. I have to do it."

"No. You don't understand! That is not the way!" Her voice had carried as the wind did.

Flashes of her at thirteen sitting in an office as the charred, ruined estate was turned over to her. The training she pushed herself to do for the next year until she could enroll in the ranger academy she had paid her way into. She pushed herself through all that hurt and those memories to get to the top of her class. The others whispered, saying she had killed her parents. They pushed her into walls, and she would become too violent as she went through her drills and tests. The final exam was in the middle of the sparring match with the biggest prick at the academy. Rain poured down in buckets, the heavy monsoon rains of Askra Falls. She recalled the sound of all that water pounding against the walls and the glass—pounding against her heart. It all crashed down on her again, and that magic came out and hurt her opponent. Magic was banned in the school. They said rangers do not use mage or witch magic. They didn't want to let her in. They suggested Iris Glade Academy for mages would be better suited for a 'sea witch', as they called her. She'd never be a mage. She didn't want to be a witch, and she didn't want to be a Gaffney. Six years had gone by in a second.

Dishonorably disenrolled. Iris Glade wouldn't take her any-way with this. As she left the school, Harper was furious at every-thing. She hated her bloodline. She knew she could never outrun it either, but still tried to.

"Please, Harper. I cannot watch this happen again. Please." Layla's voice felt as though it had cupped Harper's jaw and turned her attention back to the woman in front of her.

She was so beautiful, but Layla was telling her to go, not to stay. Layla would be horrified if she knew all that had happened to her and how piss-poor Harper had handled it all. The angry sea witch did not belong. You couldn't run from your blood-line. You just had to bury the name and hope no one ever dug it up again. She would rip herself free of the Gaffney name right now. She leveled her gaze at Layla.

"If you want to stay here, then stay, Layla. I need to get that flower and keep moving. I cannot let my past catch up to me, even here. They will hunt me down, Askra Falls, Renton, this damned forest king. I have to run."

"Harper, please! That is the wrong way."

She did not listen to the woman who had caught her eye, whom she found a curiosity toward. No, Harper Gaffney did not listen to Layla. Harper Gaffney only listened to her pounding heart—the frantic hooves of the wild elk running through the fields, their bones glowing brightly under the moonlight. Her thoughts ran as franticly as they did. Yet as those thoughts raced, she saw all that she had lost, and all the horrors of this wretched forest. She saw her home, Gaffney Manor, the market in Askra Falls, and her mom and dad holding her hand. She saw small hands swirling salty ocean water in the sand, creating an orb, her mother smiling as she watched, and her father laughing and clapping with glee.

The old woman's song played in her ears. *How it swells and breaks . . . Little coastal witch.*

Then Harper saw Layla in front of her. The hurt on her face tugged violently at her own heart, and a sob threatened to rip out of her.

"You need to turn back if you want to keep moving. This is not the way out of this forest. The moon flower you see down there is his beacon. You know this. He cannot steal that which is unclaimed. If you wish to flee, you must turn back," Layla said with hurt in her voice.

Turning around, Harper took in Lassen Peak and the shadows it cast over the forest. The moon illuminated those stubborn snow patches that clung to the ground despite the hot air.

This shadow brought all these terrors to life. It created the darkness that lived among the cedars and the firs.

Her heart began to pound again. The coastal witch was so far from the coast. She was so far from home, yet home was gone.

She could not return there ever again, for she would be cast out once more. The pounding in her heart grew louder with each beat, as if it was getting closer. The elk drew nearer. No, it was only one elk pounding into the earth. The large elk made of bones and its rider made of shadow loomed nearby. The forest king's mount was hunting her, the coastal witch. He did not have one in his collection. Why would he?

"He will ride toward the beacon, knowing you are there. You must run, Harper."

Harper met Layla's sad gaze. The moon flower pulsed with a white glow under the moonlight. A beacon, a beacon of a new start. All she needed to do was grab it.

The rules replayed in her head. Don't touch it with your hands. Use your blade to dig it out. You have gloves on. Use your cloak.

She noticed Layla fighting back a cry as she walked toward her. How gracefully this woman walked. *It was almost ethereal*, Harper noted.

"You will be ok. He cannot hurt you as long as you stay away from the beacons. You will find your way. You will be ok. Let's go. Let's get you out of here," Layla said in sad resignation, as though she were letting something go.

Something was not right. Harper could not figure out what this feeling was that cut through the pounding of the elk's hooves and her pounding heart. The ground was not that far below. She had done obstacles similar to running down a ledge many times in her ranger training. She would get that flower, and she would get that bounty.

With one short inhale in affirmation, Harper spun around and ran past Layla, who gasped.

"Harper! No!"

Layla's scream was nearly blocked out by her steps echoing through her body as she sprinted. Dry, dusty soil created a haze, and the ground was hard to make out.

Her boot landed on rock, and as if the dry soil gave the rock a shove, her boots were no longer on the ground.

A gasp turned into a cough from the dust in the air as her back hit the ground. Then her chest hit the ground. Then her back again. Frantically trying to grab anything at all, her palms stung as they scraped across small rocks and twigs. Ignoring the cracking sound and sudden sharp pain she felt in her leg, all Harper focused on was stopping her rolling down the cliffside. The cracking sound radiated in her head, pairing with the night sky flipping in and out of sight as though it were on a timelapse.

Only when Layla's frantic cries followed her into the void did Harper focus on something other than her fall. Yet, she could not slow herself. The pain started to subside, and she wondered, hoped, that she was past the worst of the fall. Her vision began to grow darker than the shadow the mountain created. Sounds were muffled. Then her body jerked with the sudden impact of something hard, as if she broke through a barrier of some kind. It did not hurt, though. She couldn't feel, see, nor hear anything here. This was nothing. She was nothing in this space.

I n what felt like mere seconds, Harper opened her eyes with a gasp and tried to push herself up. Some force held her to the ground as she glanced up at the moon. Struggling as though she were fighting the krakens of the deep seas trying to hold her down, she broke free and ran, not daring to look back.

If Harper Gaffney had looked back, she would have realized what had happened. She would see she had accomplished the task she set out to do when she fled the seaside town that swirled in rumors. She would see that she had little else to do.

"Harper!" That voice called to her. That voice that sparked her curiosity, that made her feel as though everything would be ok. Yet, it wasn't ok. That voice did not seem to want to really leave here. "Wait."

"No!" Harper was moving faster than she knew she could, and she reached the moon lotus. Dropping to her knees with her gloves on, she could finally get this flower. The lore might be right, but she'd be damned if she was going to be one of the souls that the damned king stole. "I'm getting out of here. I'm sorry, Layla!" she huffed.

Her hand dug into the earth, and confusion began to cascade all over her. She could not lift the flower; she could not move the earth. Eyes widening, Harper feared this was an illusion. Another trick of this horrible place. This horrible place was masked in alluring magic. She could not blame Layla for not taking more urgency to leave this place, but she would not become another soul on that king's shelf. She would not be stolen. Harper realized Layla never seemed afraid of him, and she wanted to stay in this place.

The snap of a twig made the stampede in her head stop. For a split second she noticed the pounding was not in her head, nor her chest. In fact, she could feel nothing in her chest. It echoed in her head against nothing. That split second was all but forgotten when that looming figure of starless sky approached. He had narrowed black eyes with the shimmer of sapphire against his moonlight-white skin. An obsidian crown sat atop his head of wavy black hair that flowed with his billowing black robes. They may as well have been made of shadows.

And as he approached, Harper found herself not moving, not being able to. It was not fear or defiance that bound her, she realized. Nor was it the Kraken or whatever entity had bound her before. No, this was a sorrow that formed deep inside her. Despite the sorrow, she could somehow see beyond it, and a comfort waited to embrace her.

Too much. Harper was processing too much. She could hardly function, and when she met his eyes as he leaned down, all she could do was stare back.

The forest king cupped her chin, yet she did not scream or flinch. He smirked at her. "What a clever little coastal witch you are. One line ceases to exist, yet the shadow of the mountain gets more crowded." His words coiled around her as if they were mist gracing her ears. He let her chin go and simply walked away.

The bindings and chains holding her there shattered, and she got up to run. "Screw all of this!" she said, running fast until she skidded to a halt. The realization of what had happened, of the king's words, hit, and a sob wrenched through her.

A man in a Renton guard uniform sighed and shook his head.

"Unfortunate. She was young too," he said, then hoisted Harper's lifeless body onto the cart. The brown mare was spooked as it stared right at Harper. It let out a whinny and stomped a hoof, indicating a sense of urgency. The guard grabbed the reins and walked right past Harper. She tilted her head at the lifeless body on the cart. She observed the fresh blood from the skull that had been fractured. She studied the broken spine and leg and the palms that had been nearly skinned. Her battered weapons were tossed haphazardly on the cart.

A lifeless body. Harper's lifeless body. Dead. Harper Gaffney was dead. She had died in that fall. Layla tried to reach for her, tried to stop her, tried to save her, and now she was dead. She collapsed and sobbed. Her tears fell, illuminating the ground with a pulse of ocean-blue light, for that ocean magic still raged inside her. As she cried her sorrows, she could feel someone approaching. She didn't bother looking up. What difference did it make? It was one of the living who couldn't see her, or it was the king coming to collect her. Or it would be Layla, worried and searching for her, never knowing what had happened.

Her body went rigid as she felt someone sit next to her and place a hand on her back.

"It will be ok." Layla's soft voice caressed her ears.

Harper gazed up at the woman, her smile soft and warm.

"Would you like to stay with me tonight, now that we are no longer different?"

"What?" Harper gasped.

"He cannot steal that which is unclaimed." Layla's smile shrank.

"My body claimed my soul, and I lost it! You are immune because you died here!"

Layla nodded and took Harper's hand. "Let's go. I will tell you the story over tea. The village I live in belongs to the entity that makes Lassen Peak, not the king. Our final resting place is in the shadow of Lassen, not as trophies for the king to marvel at."

The two walked toward a small village where cottages and houses were filled with warm lights, their hearths billowing. Living within were those who fell before and became claimless.

About the Author

Kelly Virens is a fantasy author with a love of all things trees, oceans, hiking, fantasy, and fae. Born and raised in San Diego, California, with a two-year teaching stint in Japan, she relocated to Northern California to find home in all the amazing areas nearby. When she is not writing, she is usually off hiking or exploring somewhere in the Northern California region, where she finds inspiration. Following a hike, she always stops by a nearby bookstore and a coffee shop. Her imagination is usually dreaming and scheming new things to write, draw, or make.

Follow along with her explorations on Instagram
with her personal account @fireflirt and
bookstagram @KellyVirensBooks

Kandy Apple Karma

Brandee Paschall

Content/trigger warnings:

———◈———

Blood and murder

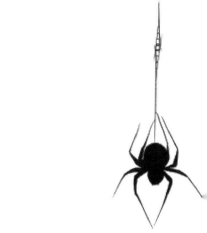

Sugar maple and dogwood leaves covered the hardened ground, and the jack-o'-lanterns had yet to be lit. The small trailer park located in upstate New York was covered in various shades of crimson, amber, and auburn colors, signifying that autumn had truly come in full force that year. On the back most street of the park laid a small two-bedroom trailer hosting a family of four, the Robertsons. Orange and purple lights were strung from the roof in a disproportionate pattern and two carved pumpkins sat on the front porch, one with an almost perfectly shaped face and the other with a messy-looking face that resembled Edvard Munch's 'The Scream.'

Inside the house was the youngest child, Leigh, who had already returned from school that afternoon and was lying on the living room floor at the end of the long hallway that led to the bedrooms. Her mother had already begun preparing for dinner in the kitchen. Leigh kicked her feet back and forth as she colored a picture for her sister of the pretty doll that sat in a rocking chair at the end of the hall, the doll's hair laying in long brown waves and her skin shining like porcelain. The young girl's mother had told them it was their grandmother's doll and needed to be carefully handled, so in the chair it laid, never to be played with and only admired. The young girl's picture hardly looked like the doll though. As much as she might've tried, the picture looked more like a Sesame Street character than a perfectly preserved doll.

As the clock struck away another hour, the front door swung open with a noisy creak and the eldest child, Lynn, appeared in the doorway carrying her worn, overfilled JanSport backpack with only one strap over her thin shoulders. Lynn stayed at school later that day for cheer practice.

Leigh sprung from the floor, running for her older sister. Although there was an eight-year difference between the sixteen-year-old and eight-year-old, they were as close as siblings could be. They did not fight, they did not ignore each other as siblings tended to do. No, these two sisters had a love unlike any pair ever seen.

"Did you have a good day at school, Leigh?" asked Lynn. "Finish all your homework?" Lynn scuffed up the young girl's curly brunette hair as she entered the room and sat her backpack under the coat hook beside the door.

"Yup, it's all done!" Leigh exclaimed, hopping from one foot to the other.

The eldest sister laughed. "Are you excited about something?" she asked, tapping a finger to her chin. "Perhaps there's a good movie showing tonight?"

The little girl shook her head no, still smiling.

"No? Is there a snake on the back porch again?" Lynn asked, a hand on her hip.

The girl pursed her lips, and mocked her sister's position. "It's Halloween, Lynn."

Lynn smirked. "Is it? I had no idea."

"You promised to take me trick-or-treating, Lynnie!" little Leigh shouted.

Lynn laughed, "I know, I know! I will, but I promised some of my friends they could join us. Is that okay?"

"Who?" Leigh asked, crossing her arms and squinting her eyes at Lynn.

"Ash, Maria, Joe, and Liam," Lynn said, smirking at her younger sister's attitude.

Leigh sighed. "I guess that's okay."

"You guess?" Lynn asked, giggling, "Well, we will get you changed into your costume after dinner and go, okay?"

"Okay," Leigh said, hopping up and down with excitement.

Halloween was the girls' absolute favorite holiday, ranking even above Christmas. They would spend the entire month watching spooky movies, eating candy-corn, and meticulously planning out their costumes.

The two sisters sat down on the couch as they finished the dinner their mother had prepared. She had found some pumpkin shaped pasta for the occasion and had made a Halloween version of Leigh's favorite dinner, tomato soup and noodles. Their father called it, 'Poor Man's Spaghetti.'

The television speakers let out a loud scream as one of the killers chased after their victim.

The girl's mother appeared from the kitchen then, a dish towel in hand, "Lynn, she's too young for this movie! She'll have nightmares later!" she scolded, grabbing the remote to change the TV to the news station.

"I'm not too young, Mama!" Leigh yelled. "I love scary movies!"

Their mother grimaced. "You're the only eight years old I know that enjoys all this spooky stuff. But either way it's getting dark outside. Go get your costume out and Lynn will come help you zip your dress up."

Leigh huffed but turned quickly to run down the hall toward the bedroom she shared with Lynn, shouting a, 'Hello!' to the porcelain doll as she went.

Lynn grimaced. "I hate that stupid doll. It just stares down the hallway with those beady, dead eyes."

"An eight-year-old that likes scary movies, and a six-teen-year-old who is afraid of dolls. You two are so alike but so different at the same time," their mother said, shaking her head as she laughed.

The TV got louder suddenly as the news anchor started his new story about crime in the city being at an all-time high and an escaped convict on the loose. The co-anchor spouted off about not canceling your Halloween activities, because safety measures were being taken and authorities believed the convict would be heading south into New Jersey. The mother frowned at the television. "Make sure you are both back by ten tonight, and don't leave the neighborhood."

"We won't. We'll be careful," Lynn promised before kissing her mother's cheek and following her sister's path down the hallway to their room.

F our feet kicked back and forth under the porch as the girls waited for Lynn's friends to arrive. Leigh frowned at her older sister, whose brown curls were pulled into a high ponytail and wore black ripped jeans, a white t-shirt, and a black leather jacket. It wasn't much of a Halloween costume, but Lynn had told her she was supposed to be a 'motorcycle chick.' However, the costume wasn't very different from Lynn's normal attire. Leigh glanced down at her own costume and adjusted her fluffy tutu made from black tulle. She'd chosen to dress as a witch this year, complete with purple sparkly tights, a pointy black hat, and a witch's broom that stood taller than Leigh herself.

Leaves crunched as Leigh lifted her head and Lynn's best friend, Ash, walked up the driveway with three other teenagers that Lynn didn't recognize. Leigh smiled widely at Ash, who was dressed head to toe in black with cat ears sticking out of her long blonde hair. A long black tail swished behind her as she walked, almost like a real cat.

"Hey, squirt!" Ash said, poking Leigh in the side playfully.

Leigh giggled, swatting her hand away and hopping off the porch. "Hi, Ash! Your costume is so awesome!"

Ash smiled widely as her eyes glanced down at Leigh's costume before she looked at her best friend's lack of costume and raised a brow at her. The three strangers behind Ash snickered down at Leigh and her sparkly tights.

"So what's the plan for tonight, Lynn?" the red-haired girl asked as she leaned against the blond-haired boy's chest. The other boy stared at Lynn with a lopsided grin, his black hair almost hiding his eyes from how long it was.

Lynn blushed at him before turning her attention back to the redhead. "Maria, I told you and Joe earlier today that we were taking Leigh trick-or-treating."

The redhead, Maria, frowned down at Leigh in distaste. "I thought you were kidding. Aren't you a little old for trick-or-treating, kid?"

Lynn grounded her teeth, nervously glancing toward the boy with black hair.

Leigh cocked her hip and crossed her arms. "Aren't you a little young to have all those hickeys on your neck?"

The other teens burst out laughing and Ash held out a fist to Leigh, who pounded her own fist against it. Maria glared at the little girl, but kept her mouth shut.

"We better get going if we're going to get the good candy before it's gone," the black-haired boy said, coming to stand beside Lynn.

The group headed down the street closest to the Robertson's trailer, Maria and Joe in the lead, Ash and Leigh in the middle, and Lynn and the black-haired boy in the rear.

"Thanks, Liam," Lynn whispered, reaching her hand out to interlock her fingers with his.

"No problem, Lynn. I have a little brother, I get it," Liam said, using his free hand to mess with his long hair.

"He doesn't go trick-or-treating anymore?" Lynn asked, tucking a stray hair behind her ear as she watched the group in front of her reach the first house.

"Nah. He stopped last year. Kinda sad, really." Liam said, staring at Leigh's broom as it dragged against the pavement.

Leigh stopped at the bottom of the steps, turning to stare at Lynn expectantly.

Maria cackled. "Well, what are you waiting for, kid? Go get your candy so we can move on! We don't have all night."

Leigh frowned at her and looked at Lynn with hopeful eyes. Maria raised a brow at Lynn, a smirk on her face. Lynn stared back at Maria and glanced at Joe, who was holding in his laughter. "Go ahead, Leigh. You don't need me to walk up to the door."

Leigh's eyes widened, and she moved her lips to object, but saw that her sister had turned her attention to her other friends. Liam glanced between the siblings with concerned eyes.

"Do you want me to go with you?" Ash whispered to Leigh with a grimace.

Leigh glanced at her momentarily before returning her attention to her older sister, tears welled up in her eyes before she blinked them away and straightened her shoulders. "No, I can go alone, I guess," Leigh muttered before grabbing the handrail and walking up the steps to the porch and rang the doorbell. An older woman with snowy white hair answered the door with a toothy grin and a bowl filled with large candy bars.

"There you go, dearie," Mrs. Phelps said as she dropped a Hershey's bar into Leigh's bag.

"Thank you," Leigh said, eyes wide as she stared down into her bag at the huge score she'd gotten. Liam had been right about getting the good candy before it was gone.

Leigh trotted down the steps and into the street where the group waited, and without saying anything she continued onto the next house. She didn't even spare Lynn a glance. Lynn sighed as she watched her little sister led the group to the next few houses and go up to each door alone. She became more and more nauseous as the night moved on. Guilt ate at her like a dog with a chew toy.

"What's wrong, Lynn?" Liam asked her, noticing as she held her stomach and grimaced as her sister walked up another set of steps alone.

"I shouldn't have made her go alone. We're supposed to be trick-or-treating together. It's our favorite holiday. I feel like a terrible sister," Lynn whispered, staring down at her shoes as she twisted her toes in the dirt.

"Just apologize," Liam said, smiling. "I'm sure she'll forgive you."

"You're right. I shouldn't let Maria' pressure me like that." Lynn sighed. "I wouldn't want Leigh to let some bully run all over her."

Liam squeezed her hand before dropping it and trotting up to Ash to continue walking down the street. They were about halfway through the trailer park at this point. Lynn walked past the group to where her sister walked alone and wrapped her right arm around Leigh's shoulders to embrace her in a side hug.

"I'm sorry, Leigh. It wasn't cool of me to abandon you like that," Lynn said. "Do you want me to go with you to the door from now on?"

Leigh clenched her jaw and fists and stared ahead as they walked, choosing not to answer.

Lynn sighed. "I really am sorry, Lee-Lee. Please forgive me?" Lynn begged, but Leigh still did not answer, so Lynn asked, "What if I wear your hat? Then we can both be witches?"

Leigh snorted. "But you're a biker chick,"

Lynn grinned widely; she'd cracked her. "I can be a biker witch. They're all the rage now, you know." Lynn bumped her hip against Leigh playfully.

Leigh giggled. "Yeah, right. Don't you want to look 'cool' in front of your friends?"

Lynn frowned. "I did. But they're not very nice friends, so I shouldn't care what they think. I do care what you think, though."

Leigh pondered what Lynn had said. "Ash and Liam are nice friends," Leigh stated.

"Yes, they are." Lynn smiled, taking Leigh's pointy witch hat and placing it on top of her head.

"Is Liam your boyfriend or a friend that's a boy?" Leigh asked suddenly.

Lynn raised a brow at her little sister. Maybe she was letting her watch too many movies. "I haven't decided yet," she said.

"You haven't decided, or he hasn't asked?" Ash asked, popping her head between the two sisters.

Lynn shoved her friend back playfully and rolled her eyes. "Let's just get to the next house.

"Yes, can we *please* get this over with! I'm tired of babysitting the toddler," Maria yelled from behind them.

"Shut up, Maria," Liam barked from the back of the group, causing Maria to scoff and glare ahead.

"I'm really getting tired of her and her shitty attitude," Ash murmured.

"Me too, but if I don't suck it up and deal, I'll have no chance at co-captain in the spring. I told her we were going trick-or-treating, so I'm not sure why she's acting like such a twat," Lynn said, glaring at the red head who was inspecting her nails.

The group continued on to the next street over, where some of the houses' lights had started to turn off for the night. There would most likely be nothing left but toothbrushes and dental floss soon, little Leigh thought to herself. A street light flicked ominously over a slumped figure, and the group slowed as they passed, keeping a wide berth between them and the mysterious form. Leigh inspected the figure as she was the closest, noticing the oozing red liquid that lined the person's neck and dripped down onto his lap. The figure suddenly twitched frantically before returning to its frozen position against the light pole.

"Cool costume!" Leigh whispered to Ash and Lynn, pointing toward the flickering light casting shadows over the figure.

"Cool? More like creepy as hell!" Maria whisper-shouted. She and Joe had moved closer to the group.

"Think they used pig's blood?" Liam asked with a wry smile.

Leigh giggled. "They have fake blood in the stores now. You don't have to use pig's blood."

"Oh my God, Liam. You and that little brat are both freaks!" Maria shrieked, grabbing Joe's hand and dragging him ahead of the group to the next house. Liam rolled his eyes at the drama queen.

Ash grimaced. "Shouldn't someone go make sure it's fake, and that the guy isn't actually bleeding?"

"Don't you watch the movies?" Liam asked.

"You NEVER investigate. That's how you die," Leigh said matter-of-factly.

They stopped next to the porch with Maria mumbling about how her Halloween had been ruined by an 'annoying toddler.'

Lynn rolled her eyes. "Come on, Leigh. Let's get some more candy," she said as she guided her sister up the steps.

The night continued like that, with Leigh and Lynn collecting candy and occasionally dental floss. One house gave Leigh a five-dollar bill after running out of candy from the group of kids ahead of them. Leigh didn't complain, though.

Maria continued to complain the entire time, wanting to ditch Leigh at home so that the 'grown ups' could go roll some houses with toilet paper. As the group approached the last house on the street, an old mansion came into view. It was a two-story home that had been white at one point, but the paint had long since peeled leaving the house looking more like something out of a scary movie. It had been there long before the trailer park had been, and couldn't be torn down no matter how much the residents of the park complained. It was some sort of historic landmark or something.

Leigh and Lynn would always make a game of guessing what had happened to its previous occupants, like if the house had been haunted by an old widow whose husband had died in some war. Or maybe a masked murderer was hiding in it, like one of those old John Carpenter movies. Nobody really knew what happened to the people that used to live in it; the house had been abandoned for as long as the Robertson's had lived there. However, as the group started to pass in front of the old house, the front porch light flickered on, and a jack-o'-lantern glowed faintly.

"I didn't realize someone had moved into the old place," Lynn pondered. "I always imagined the floors were falling in or something."

"Me too. It just looks so unlivable," Ash agreed, adjusting the cat ears atop her head.

"Well, they have a jack-o'-lantern. Let's go check it out," Liam said, walking up to the gate to open its door. It let out a loud squeal as it opened, causing everyone in the group to cringe.

"Spooky," Leigh said, grinning as she walked through its opening.

Liam smirked down at the eight-year-old. She was a brave kid. The group headed up the long driveway that led to the front porch with only minimal complaints from the red-headed peanut gallery and her blond-haired boyfriend, Joe. As the door came into view, so did a rocking chair seated on the left side of the door. Sitting in the chair was a life-size figure dressed in a deep-sea diving suit. The round copper helmet was covered in scratches and patches of mud and various shades of mold. The helmet's window revealed nothing and resembled the blacked-out window of a car. Leigh stopped in front of the diver and squinted her eyes at it, before shrugging her shoulders and reaching for the doorbell next to the front door. Nothing happened.

"The doorbell probably doesn't work, Leigh. You'll have to knock," Lynn said, staring apprehensively at the diver. Hell of a decoration, she thought.

Leigh knocked repeatedly on the door and the group waited for someone to answer. A couple minutes passed, with each member of the group taking a turn to knock louder and louder on the door. Lynn continued to stare at the diver, frowning at the musty scent that was resonating off its weathered fabric. Whoever had bought this house had taken the scary aspect of their home way too seriously. Spiderwebs covered each corner of the porch, with spiders of every size and color scurrying through their webs. Whoever had bought this house hadn't thought about the diseases that these insects could carry, and could possibly give to the costumed children if they'd been bitten.

"Can we go already? Nobody is coming to the door!" Maria shouted, stomping her foot and causing a few snapping sounds to crackle through the porch and shake its foundation.

"Don't do that, Maria. This house is old and I really don't feel like paying to fix it," Ash said, placing a hand on her cocked hip.

"Whatever," Maria said, placing her hand in front of her forehead as she made an L-shape with her thumb and pointer finger.

Joe walked up to the diver, leaning down to stare into the black window of the copper mask. "Wonder how much they paid for this hunk of junk?" he asked.

"I would leave that alone if I were you," Liam advised.

"They probably found it at the dump and thought it matched the house," Maria said, snorting.

Lynn, Ash, and Liam frowned at the pair. If whoever lived in that old house was there, they were going to think the group was a bunch of rude hooligans.

"I dare you to poke it, Joe!" Maria said, laughing obnoxiously.

"No way. There's no telling what diseases this thing is covered in," Joe said, scrunching up his nose in disgust. "Hey, kid, poke it with your broom!"

Leigh frowned at the dirty diver suit and then down at her witch's broom that she and Lynn had made together. It had taken them hours to get the black ribbon tied around the broom's shaft just right, and even longer to dye the brush the correct shade of black. They had just sprayed it with silver glitter before leaving the house that night.

"No, I don't want to," Leigh said.

"What's wrong, kid? Are you scared of the dirty old diver?" Joe asked, raising his brows.

"Leave her alone, dude. If she doesn't want to do it, she doesn't have to," Liam said, crossing his arms and stepping in front of Leigh protectively.

Lynn reached for Leigh's hand, and glared at Joe and Maria. "Come on, Leigh. We can still hit a few more houses before it's time to head home."

Leigh stared at her sister's hand and then at Liam, who was still glaring at Joe. Leigh didn't want them to think she was scared, because she wasn't. She just didn't want to ruin the broom they had worked so hard on, but she guessed she could poke the diver really quick. Just to shut those bullies up.

"I'll do it." Leigh sighed, walking past Liam and Joe to stand before the musty diver.

Leigh lifted her broom with the handle facing the diver and slowly reached it out to poke the diver in the chest. The handle met a hard and stiff surface, but the diver didn't move. It was just a decoration.

"That was a weak poke," Joe laughed. "Let me do it." Joe snatched the broom from Leigh's hands and spun it around in his hands so that the brush faced away from him.

"Stop! Give me my broom back!" Leigh shouted angrily, hopping for the broom that Joe held out of reach.

Liam's eyes darkened as he stepped closer and shoved Joe. "Give her the broom, man."

"Or what?" Joe asked, glaring back before whipping the broom around to hit the diver across its copper helmet, "It's just a silly decoration—"

The diver suddenly stood from its chair, lifting its arms to wrap around Joe's shoulders, and pulling him against his chest before roaring in his ears. The entire group screamed and scurried off the porch and down the driveway. They didn't stop until they were back out of the gate and on the main road again.

Everyone turned to stare at each other with wide eyes. Ash stood hunched over with her hands on her knees, taking deep breaths. Tears were streaming down Leigh's cheeks.

"Oh, Leigh. It'll be okay!" Lynn said, dropping to her knees to wrap her arms around her whimpering little sister.

Loud laughter had the pair pulling apart, to stare at Joe, who had just exited the front gate. He snorted at the sight of the tears that were still streaming down Leigh's cheeks.

"That's what you get, you little brat. I knew you had to be scared of something, you little freak," Joe sneered.

Liam gritted his teeth, lifting his fist to punch Joe across the jaw. He pulled his fist back to throw another punch, but was stopped by Ash's hand on his shoulder. Joe glared back at Liam, holding a hand to cover what was sure to become a nasty bruise.

"He's not worth it, Liam," Ash said, "Although I'd like to throw a couple punches myself."

Maria scoffed, "You're all a bunch of freaks!" she shouted, holding her hand up to caress Joe's other cheek, "Come on, baby. I told you these guys were just a bunch of losers!"

"Hold on," Lynn said, standing from where she had been embracing Leigh, "What happened to the diver guy?"

Joe rolled his eyes. "Just the owner playing a prank, obviously. He let me go as soon as you lot started running for the hills." He snorted. "Let's go, Maria. I'm sure we can find something better to do with our time than trick-or-treat." He raised an eyebrow at her.

Maria's eyes widened, and she blushed before nodding. She turned her eyes on the rest of the group with a sneer. "Have fun with your candy, losers."

The pair walked off in the opposite direction, and Liam stared after them. His eyes were still dark with anger and his fists still clenched. Leigh stood from where she had sat on the sidewalk to cry and walked over to Liam, grabbing his hand in hers. Liam's eyes lightened when he looked down at her and smiled.

"You okay, Leigh?" he whispered, his voice still gruff with anger.

"Yeah. I'll be okay." Leigh sniffled, but smiled up at him, "Let's go get some more candy!"

Liam grinned and turned away from the retreating couple to guide the girls toward the last of the houses in the trailer park. As the group finished off the last of the houses, they discussed all of their favorite Halloween traditions, from watching spooky movies to carving pumpkins and exploring corn mazes.

Leigh was sad, knowing that the night would soon be over. It would be another three hundred and sixty-five days until next Halloween, and she already couldn't wait. She would start planning her costume as soon as she woke up. Maybe Lynn would invite Liam to come trick-or-treating next year. Leigh liked him.

As the group made their way back the way they had come, they stopped at a baby-blue colored trailer, where a single jack-o'-lantern sat on the front porch. This trailer was where the Foyer family lived. Ash walked over to the bottom step of the porch and turned around.

"Well, this is me. Thanks for letting me come trick-or-treat with you guys," Ash said, spinning her cat tail around in her hands.

Leigh ran up to her and threw her arms around her, almost knocking Ash off balance. They both giggled as Lynn came up and wrapped her arms around both of them in a group hug. Liam stood awkwardly on the side with his hands in his pockets.

"Goodnight, Ash. I'll see you at school!" Lynn shouted at her, Leigh, and Liam continued down the street toward the girls' home.

The street lights had long since turned on and without them, the group wouldn't be able to see their hands if they held them in front of their faces. Very few houses had left their porch lights on, assuming that all the trick-or-treaters had shed their costumes and gone to bed. Lynn checked her watch for the time, noting that it was half-past nine and they would need to be home soon. Liam came to walk beside her and entwined his fingers with hers.

Lynn smiled down at their hands. "I'm glad you came tonight."

"Me too. It's been . . . eventful, but interesting to be sure," Liam chuckled.

"It has. For a moment back there, I thought we had run into that escaped convict the news was blathering about. But they said he would be heading south," Lynn said.

"I don't think so," Liam said. "This is his hometown."

Lynns eyes widened as she looked at Liam. "How do you know that?"

"I looked him up after I saw the news story. I'm kind of a true crime junkie, I guess you could say," Liam said sheepishly.

Lynns shoulders tensed. "So you think he will come here, and not run south?"

Liam shrugged. "What better way to spend Halloween than to have a murder spree in your hometown."

"Maybe we should get home then." Lynn frowned at her little sister, who was pretending to ride her broom just ahead of them.

Liam chuckled. "No worries, Lynn. You are safe with me," he said, squeezing Lynn's hand. Lynn smiled at him nervously.

As they grew closer to the light pole from earlier, the group stopped in their tracks. The light continued to flicker over the paved street, some old faulty wires that nobody had bothered to fix. However, there was no longer a slumped figure leaning against the base of the pole.

"Maybe they went home?" Leigh asked, reaching for her older sister's hand.

Lynn murmured her agreement as they drew closer. Drag marks and a mysterious red liquid coated the ground, leading behind one of the trailers and continuing to who knew where. Lynn and Liam made quick eye contact, silently deciding to continue walking and pretend that they hadn't noticed the strange marks. Although the speed at which they walked did increase tremendously.

"That guy took his costume to the next level," Leigh said nonchalantly, staring back over her shoulder at the markings.

Lynn furrowed her brows. "What do you mean, Leigh?"

"He put those drag marks there to freak people out after leaning against the pole all night people were going to wonder where he went," Leigh said, shrugging.

Lynn raised a brow and looked at Liam questioningly. Liam grinned down at the eight-year-old before shrugging at Lynn. That did seem like a better explanation than somebody dragging him away, Lynn thought. Or at least she hoped that was the case . . . they really needed to get home.

"What is your favorite scary movie, Leigh?" Liam asked suddenly.

Leigh tapped her finger on her chin, squinting her eyes as she thought about his question, "I don't have a favorite, but I do love the ones with masked killers on the loose."

Lynn snorted, shaking her head in disbelief. It still amazed her that an eight-year-old could love all things spooky and wasn't afraid of what went bump in the night. Lynn grimaced as she thought of that strange porcelain doll at home that Leigh loved so much. She loved a good scary movie, but when it came to real life, Lynn would rather the spooky shit stay on the screen.

"Huh. I like those too," Liam said, smiling up at the moon in the sky. How ironic that it was in the perfect phase on Halloween. *Wonder where the werewolves are*, Liam thought. "Although, I think it is even scarier when the killer does not wear a mask, and they leave their true colors hidden beneath a false persona."

Leigh and Lynn nodded their agreement.

As the group rounded the corner and walked onto the final street that would lead to the Robertson's home, a tall dark figure emerged from behind one of the trees. It was about twenty feet in front of the group and just out of reach of the illumination that the light poles procured. The group slowed as they came closer to it and completely stopped when the figure walked onto the paved street and into the limelight. The copper shined in the parts of the helmet that weren't covered in dirt and mold, and blood dripped onto the weathered boots of the divers' suit. Hanging from the diver's hand was the decapitated head of the man they had seen leaning against the light pole.

"Guess it wasn't pig's blood," Liam whispered, a wry smile on his face.

Leigh and Lynn looked at Liam with wide eyes before looking at each other and screaming their lungs out. Lynn grabbed her sister's hand and began running in the direction they had come from, deciding that they would get home from the other street that led to their house. Eventually, Lynn picked Leigh up in her arms so that they could run quicker. Leigh stared back at the diver's helmet that had been abandoned and now laid sideways on the ground. Its occupant was no longer visible, and Liam was no longer in sight, either. *Where had they gone?* she wondered.

Lynn ran and didn't stop until she and Leigh had reached the sidewalk's edge that led to their house. She put Leigh down on the ground and grabbed her hand in hers.

"What happened to Liam?" Lynn asked, staring in the direction they had from as she heaved in as much oxygen as she could get.

Leigh shrugged, unconcerned about their friend. "I don't know, but let's go inside."

The girls walked up the yard and steps that led to their front porch, and after getting inside and locking the door, Lynn's cellphone let out a quick beep. Lynn stared down at the screen and let out a relieved sigh.

"Liam made it back to his house," Lynn breathed, "and he called the police."

"Must have been some sort of prank," Leigh said, shrugging. "Right?"

"You're right. A prank, that makes sense," Lynn said, nodding. "Let's go to bed. It's almost ten."

The girls took their shoes off and left them on the mat beside the door before talking down the hallway that led to their bedroom. They both quickly changed into pajamas before lying in the bed and choosing to leave the light on for the night—at Lynn's request. Just before the girls dozed off to sleep though, Leigh walked back out the bedroom door to throw a small blanket over the porcelain doll that sat at the end of the hallway.

T he next morning, the girls were sitting on the couch in the living room eating cereal. Lynn sat cross-legged on the couch texting Liam while Leigh munched on her rainbow-colored cereal and watched the last running of *Halloweentown* before they didn't play it again for a year.

The girls' mother entered the living room from the kitchen to collect the empty bowl that Lynn had abandoned on the side table. "Did you girls have fun last night?"

The girls barely murmured an answer, preoccupied with their activities. The mother shook her head at the two girls. *What was she going to do with them?* The credits rolled on Leigh's movie, so the mother picked up the remote and changed it to their local news station. A bell rang from the kitchen before she could sit down, so the mother traveled back into the kitchen.

"Local authorities arrested a man last night dressed in a deep diver's suit. The man is thought to be escaped convict, Joey Kraven. Kraven was arrested twelve years ago on the charge of multiple murders and kidnappings, but was reported as having escaped yesterday morning. Kraven was located late last night in his childhood home, which had been abandoned long ago . . . " the news anchor reported, showing a picture of the old abandoned mansion the group had visited the night before.

"Holy crap!" Lynn shouted

"Cool!" Leigh shouted at the same time.

The news anchor continued, "In related news, two teens were reported missing this morning from upstate New York. Sixteen-year-olds Maria Hudson and Joe Valentino were last seen yesterday before leaving their homes for Halloween related activities. Authorities believe serial killer, Joey Kraven, may be responsible for these kidnappings but have not ruled out other causes at this time. More on this and other news after this break . . . "

Lynn's eyes widened, and tears welled up in her eyes. "Mom!" she yelled, jumping off the couch and running into the kitchen.

Leigh stared at the TV as it changed to commercials with a smirk on her face. That's karma for you, she thought. Bullies were always the ones to die in the movies. A light knock on the door pulled Leigh from her thoughts, and she walked over to open the door. Liam stood in the doorway with a smile on his face. Lynn rushed into the room.

"Oh my God, Liam! Did you see the news?" Lynn shouted, tears streaming down her cheeks.

"I did. How crazy is that?" Liam said, shaking his head in disbelief.

Lynn threw her arms around Liam and sobbed into his chest as Liam hugged her. Leigh stood behind her, noting that Liam was in the same clothes from the night before. Leigh stared down at the cuffs of his jeans and smirked at the sight of blood stains. She looked up into Liam's smirking face as he pulled his sleeves down to hide the blood that was on his wrists.

Leigh grinned at Liam. "I guess there are all kinds of masks."

About The Author

B randee Paschall is a paranormal and fantasy romance author with a love for all things that go bump in the night. She is the author of the paranormal romance novel *Still Waters*, the first installment from *The Keepers of The Sacred Series*, filled with elemental magic, werewolves, and more. She is honored to be a part of this bone-chilling anthology, as she has always been a lover of horror, thrills, and gore. It is her beloved tradition to fill her entire spooky season with as many haunted houses and scary movies as she can. As such, the first person she dedicated this short story to was Wes Craven, the American film director and producer that brought serial killers Freddy Krueger and Ghostface to the big screen. The second person she dedicated this story to is her sister, Kristina, because without her, this story could not have been possible. Although most of this story was fictional, the two sisters and the diver were not...

Moral of the story: Don't poke the diver with your broom, and never let the bullies win.

Keep up with Brandee's writing journey and get all the details on her upcoming projects by following her socials and signing up for her newsletter! Below is her Linktree which will lead you to her: TikTok, Instagram, author newsletter, website, and more!

linktr.ee/brandee_paschall_books

Resut

Emma Jane Lounsbury

Content/trigger warnings:

Body horror, ritualistic violence,
references to sexual scenarios

Heru wakes up to hands running down his chest. Fingernails skate through the hair on his torso, and he shivers slightly. He's floating in the gooey space between sleep and consciousness where everything is hazy and soft. He doesn't remember Cleo planning to come over tonight, but maybe Danny let her in on his way to work.

A fingernail catches on the delicate skin of his nipple, and instead of continuing on, it digs in. Heru tries to flinch away from Cleo's fingers, only to find that he's unable to move.

That's the first sign that something is wrong—Cleo isn't one for midnight bondage.

The second alarm ringing in Heru's head comes from the utter absence of any odor of garlic.

Heru and Danny have been sharing an apartment for a year and a half now. And there's only one downside to the spacious two-bedroom they share just within city limits. Its placement above an Italian restaurant means that it *always* smells like garlic. Always.

Between the lack of garlic and the nails digging crescent moons into his skin, Heru is sure he's about to have one hell of a lucid dream. Too bad about the sleep paralysis holding him still.

When the fingers that evidently don't belong to Cleo start gouging into the flesh between his rib bones, he blinks his eyes open. *Might as well see what this dream has to offer.* Based on the feminine hands and immobility, Heru assumes he's about to enjoy his very first lucid sex dream.

When Heru has finally blinked enough for his eyes to focus, the scene isn't as expected.

While he is indeed shirtless and bound, the three women before him don't appear ready to get wet or wild. They're in white, shapeless clothes better suited for a convent than the orgy of his dreams. *Perhaps they're wearing robes of some kind?* Heru can only hope he'll find nothing beneath the amorphous linen gowns.

The woman directly in front of him has impossibly long brown hair that's woven into some sort of braid that wraps around her head. Her umber skin looks smooth and soft to the touch. She appears to be close in age to Heru, and he wonders if he can dream-will her to lose her white wrappings.

He squints his eyes at her and focuses on willing the ugly garment to disappear. After what feels like minutes of concentration, he speaks. "Is that considered a robe or a dress?"

The young woman—Agatha, he's decided she looks like an Agatha—stares at him. Agatha pulls her hands from his body and turns away without a word.

Without the distraction of fingers on bare skin, Heru has the chance to survey the setting of his dream. Unfortunately, the scene appears more 'ritualistic temple sacrifice' than the 'girls gone wild' mood he prefers.

He is in a huge room that he can only describe as the center of . . . something. His view allows for him to see the perimeter of the room as though he's raised above the rest of the area. The walls are broad and solid and appear to be made of some type of stone. *Sandstone? Maybe limestone?* Heru's job in pharmaceutical marketing hasn't given him much knowledge of architecture.

The walls are a dusty tan, and Heru thinks he can make out symbols and shapes in red and black, curling around the space. There are a number of obscenely wide stone columns near the perimeter of the room that appear strong enough to withstand the test of time. A smattering of tables sit nearby but none close enough to reach. The torches on the walls cast the temple in a golden glow that Heru would describe as romantic in any other scenario.

Though, perhaps there's still hope that one of the women might be interested in a lucid dream romp . . .

The woman Heru named Agatha is arranging something on a table several feet away from him. One of the other women approaches her, and they whisper words he can't understand.

"What's the plan here, ladies?"

All three women ignore him. When he cranes his neck, trying to decipher their mutterings, he finds that what he assumed was sleep paralysis is actually a series of metal bindings. They are clamped around his wrists, ankles, and waist and tether him snugly to . . . an altar. Like a pig at a roast or an offering for sacrifice. The bindings curve and swirl around his body and then appear to be secured directly into the altar. An altar with built-in bindings . . .

Lovely. Why can't I have boring dreams with orgies or flying? Or flying orgies . . .

Heru's attention is brought promptly back to his bindings when one of the women starts rolling up the cuffs of his sweatpants. He tucks his chin to his chest, watching her. She's wearing a teal-colored bracelet that distinguishes her from the other two women. Heru decides to name her Lagatha. He's not feeling particularly creative.

Lagatha shares the same glowing umber skin and dark brown hair as Agatha. Her hair is braided around the crown of her head, though it doesn't seem to twist around nearly as many times as Agatha's. When Lagatha leans in to inspect his ankle, her head tilts and the glow from the torches catches on her braids and shines back at Heru. It's as though her hair has been brushed with powdered gold that shimmers and shines in the torchlight.

Her fingernails skim up his calves as she rolls his pant legs up. Heru attempts to suppress a shiver but fails miserably. Cleo usually remembers how ticklish his legs are and stays away. He still feels a little guilty for that first time that they discovered he tends to kick out like a cranky donkey when tickled.

Lagatha doesn't know about his tendency to flail when tickled, so her fingers don't stop their delicate glides up his legs. Heru squirms on the altar and grits his teeth.

"Could you, uh—" Heru tries to flinch away from her hands without success. "You rolled my pants up. Can you stop already? I know you have me restrained and all, but I don't want to kick you."

The look Lagatha gives him is utterly unimpressed, and Heru wonders if she's in charge rather than Agatha. He can't decide which is worse—Agatha's sharp fingernails or Lagatha's calf tickles.

For a dream where he's bound, immobile, and being attended to by three different women, this certainly isn't turning out the way he'd hoped.

"Unless you plan to remove them entirely? In which case, please continue!"

Lagatha doesn't respond, but the way she's eyeing his exposed ankles feels . . . predatory. There's nothing particularly interesting about them. Heru doesn't have any birthmarks or crooked toes.

"Do you speak English?" Heru asks, simply out of curiosity. The only thing worse than a lucid dream about being tortured by women wearing sheets would be if he couldn't even talk to them. Heru likes to believe that he's excellent at speaking.

Lagatha ignores him entirely, and he drops his head back to the stone altar. His head hits with a dull *crack,* and it stings more than expected. He winces. "Shit. That hurt."

None of the women pay him attention, so he returns to his goal of flirting with Lagatha. He isn't in a position to be picky, so he's happy to settle for whichever of the three is the closest.

"It's okay if you don't. I can teach you English. I've been told I'm excellent with my mouth," Heru continues his one-sided conversation with Lagatha as though he hasn't just accidentally given himself brain damage.

Can you get brain damage in a dream? Surely, you'd wake up first.

Lagatha lets out a little huff as she rearranges objects on a nearby table, just beyond Heru's vision. "Ahah! You do speak English!" Heru proclaims with a sense of victory.

Heru knows women. He knows that his dark curls, golden skin, and charming words can win over most women—and some men—on his best days. Bound to a stone altar in a strange dream doesn't typically qualify for the best of his days, but he's resourceful if nothing else.

Lagatha returns to the altar with a small pot and what appears to be a paintbrush. Her hair is still shimmering, and Heru wonders if she's going to paint his to match. He'd be okay with that.

"Ooh, kinky! Though I'd be remiss if I didn't warn you that I'm awfully ticklish. I'd greatly appreciate it if you could steer clear of anything below my knees."

Lagatha meets his gaze with her own and she doesn't look nearly as amused as he'd prefer.

"They go on the hands, feet, and chest." Lagatha's voice is melodious, and while Heru can't place her accent, it sounds familiar. Her vowels are stilted and hesitant. As though the shapes are unfamiliar to her.

"Sorry, Lagatha. What goes where?" Heru has no idea what she's talking about, and he only hopes there aren't *more* bindings coming. Surely, he's restrained enough for whatever the women have planned?

Lagatha dips the paintbrush into the small pot, and when she pulls it back out, the tip is stained a shimmering vermilion.

When she starts painting a swirl at the heel of his left foot, Heru jolts and attempts to move as much as the altar will allow. Which isn't much. His restraints are tight and unyielding. Metal bites into the thin skin of his wrists and ankles, sharp and warm.

Between the unforgiving restraints, the stone bench, the foreign women in their robes, and now the body paint, the mood is growing increasingly dark. At best, the women need him for a mundane ritual; at worst, he's about to be sacrificed.

"Is that really necessary? This is quite uncomfortable." The soft caresses of the paintbrush twist and flick against the bottom of Heru's foot, and he holds his breath. There's nothing to be done. He can't move, can't escape, and even if he could, who's to know what worse things this dream could escalate to beyond just some non-consensual foot tickles?

Could another blow to the head be sufficient to end the dream?

Heru doesn't remember drinking before bed, but there must be a reason he hasn't woken up yet. *Did he go to the bar after work?* Anxiety bubbles like gas in his chest. *Maybe Lagatha can tickle him away?*

When Lagatha eventually pulls the paintbrush from his skin, Heru exhales in a huff. "Can you move on to the hand and chest part now?"

"No."

"What do you mean *no*? You're done! My whole foot is all swirly and painted. What more do you need?"

Dropping his chin as far as it will go until it's digging into his chest, Heru peeks down at his foot. From his left ankle down, every square inch is covered in vermilion shapes and patterns.

When he was a boy, Heru's mother loved taking him to the city's museum. The Egyptian Room was always her favorite. Countless childhood hours were spent with his nose pressed up against the plexiglass separating him from the preserved mummies on display. Though it's been several years since his mother's passing and even more since they visited a museum together, Heru's confident that the shapes on his left foot in shimmering red paint look a hell of a lot like hieroglyphics.

Heru glances up at Lagatha to find that Agatha and the third woman have joined her.

"Ahh, Agatha, Bagatha, lovely of you to join us. Will you be joining art class?"

He's decided to call the final woman Bagatha. Might as well continue the theme. Her clear, zaffre eyes are the only simple way to distinguish her from the other women. A deep, shining blue. Her supple, bronze skin glows under the same shapeless white robe, and her hair circles the crown of her head in a braid.

None of the women look the least bit impressed with his quips. *Have I always been this bad with women? Surely, Cleo would have laughed.*

Lagatha scoops fresh paint onto the brush and paints more hieroglyphs, this time on his right foot. Heru wonders if his feet are being decorated to match each other.

"Both feet? Is that *absolutely* necessary?"

The bindings dig into his skin again as he wiggles and flinches from the tickle torture.

Agatha and Bagatha move to stand on either side of the altar. If there was ever a time that Heru could choose to wake up, perhaps it should be now. *Is there any lingering chance that art class could still turn intimate?*

Based on the excruciating sensation of Lagatha painting Heru's right foot and the unimpressed expressions from all three women, Heru doesn't feel optimistic. This dream will likely be resigned to fall into the category of 'strange and disturbing' rather than 'fun and repeatable.'

Just when Heru can't bear the soft swirls on his right for a moment longer, Lagatha pulls the paintbrush away.

"Finally. I thought you might never finish. Having fun, are you?"

Lagatha has the audacity to roll her eyes at Heru's comment, and she shifts her gaze to Agatha. Some nonverbal communication passes between the women, and Heru doesn't bother to speculate on the topic. It's obviously him.

"I wish you would quit ignoring me. It's not every day I dream of three beautiful women with a penchant for bondage." Heru sighs dramatically. "Is this a punishment for something? Some sort of *look but don't touch* torture? Because if so, you could at least give me something more to look at." He attempts to gesture at the women's white, vast robes but can only manage to jerk his chin toward Lagatha's torso.

Agatha nods at Lagatha with a serious expression. Heru stares at the red shapes on the high stone ceiling and wills himself to wake up before this dream gets weird. *Weirder.*

It doesn't work.

Heru's not sure if he loses time or falls asleep—*can you fall asleep in a dream?* When his attention stops wandering, he finds that both Lagatha and Bagatha are painting symbols on his hands simultaneously, and . . . it's not the worst sensation. It's infinitely easier to tolerate than the delicate tickles on his feet.

The paint is cold but warms quickly on his skin. Soft, cool caresses as dual paintbrushes swirl and spin against his skin.

Heru jolts against his bindings when Agatha's voice comes from the space he can't see behind him. She must be at the head of the altar.

She's chanting something. A set of arranged words, over and over. Her voice is soft but clear. Almost coaxing.

"*Rella, Hrzana e Herus. Takai rhesh zimen!*
Resut molasol ye paqullina!"

If he wasn't trapped—on this altar, in this dream—Heru would find the sound enchanting. From his current position, the repetition is making him feel lightheaded and captivated. The words are still unfamiliar, the language unintelligible, but Heru wants to comply. Wants to offer Agatha her every desire just to release him from the altar and stop her chant.

The chanting stops when Bagatha and Lagatha step back from his now paint-covered hands.

What was it that Lagatha said earlier? '*Hands, feet, and chest?*'

"Well, are you going to do my chest or not? If not, might I suggest an alternate location? A little further south? I'll even keep my hands to myself." Heru winks at Lagatha who rolls her eyes in response. Bagatha giggles before she can stop herself.

The sharp, foreign words that Agatha throws at Bagatha do nothing to lessen the satisfaction that blooms in Heru's chest, bright and warm. *Bagatha it is, then.*

"Don't listen to her, Bagatha. You can paint me anywhere you want," Heru directs at Bagatha.

Bagatha leans over him to inspect the hand Lagatha painted, and she gives him a kind smile.

"Is it working?" Bagatha asks.

"I knew you were fluent! You've just been holding out on me this whole time then." Heru pouts.

"Is it working?" This time, Bagatha's words are directed at Agatha, ignoring Heru again.

Agatha releases a sigh so immense that Heru feels his curls wave in the breeze, tickling his forehead. "Herus, forgive me. This is the worst one yet." Her tone is weary and frustrated.

"I'll forgive you for the bindings but not the foot paint. I told her I was ticklish, but she wouldn't listen! I can't help it!"

Agatha groans and slaps a hand over Heru's mouth, silencing his complaints. She levels Lagatha with a glare.

"Are you certain this is the right one? He's decidedly annoying." Heru's protest is muffled under her palm.

Lagatha nods at the other woman, looking apologetic. "Yes. The signs were certain. Heru Iris. Twenty-second of his name. It's him." Lagatha curls her mouth down, as though answering in the affirmative is distasteful, unsavory.

Heru licks at Agatha's palm until she relents and removes it from his mouth. He wouldn't have minded if she left it a little longer. But only a little.

"Uhh, sorry to disappoint, ladies, but my name is *Heru* Jovin. Not *Herus*. My parent's names were Morris and Layla. I don't know anyone else with my name. Certainly not twenty others," Heru argues.

"Twenty-one. You are the twenty-second," Lagatha corrects.

"Right, twenty-one. Whatever. My last name isn't Iris."

Lagatha rolls her eyes, and Agatha releases another of her dramatic sighs. Only Bagatha watches Heru with the least bit of empathy.

"*Resut.* You need to remember," Bagatha implores.

Too bad I have no idea what she wants me to remember. Oh, do I know her?

"Remember what?" Heru asks. This dream isn't getting any more enjoyable the longer he's remained asleep. "Oh, I get it. This is some kind of subconscious technique, right? I forgot something, and now my dreams are trying to remind me. So what did I forget? That weird nut milk Danny drinks? Did I forget Cleo's birthday? Some repressed childhood trauma?"

Agatha slaps her hand back down over Heru's mouth before addressing Lagatha and Bagatha. "This changes nothing. We must proceed as planned. He remembers nothing."

The other women nod before moving away from the altar, but Agatha continues, "Find me a gag. I can't stand his blathering."

Heru tries to protest, but he's still muffled under Agatha's grip, and there's no sympathy to be found from the women. Not even Bagatha looks his way.

An ugly scrap of fabric gets shoved into his mouth before the women begin chanting again. Heru's burned through the adrenaline high from arguing over his name. His bare skin prickles with goosebumps and his eyelids are heavy.

I can't wait to wake up.

"R*esut.*"

Heru must have dozed off again. After the women found a gag to secure around his head, they left his line of sight for a time. It could have been minutes or hours. Maybe days. Heru finds that time passes differently in his dreams.

It's fascinating that he can still fall asleep within a dream. *I was so sure I'd wake up this time.*

"*Resut,* Herus," Bagatha whispers at his side. He rolls his head to the left to find her pulling a paintbrush away from his chest. "You need to remember."

How am I supposed to know what it is that I can't remember?

He can't see what Bagatha painted on his chest without a mirror, but whatever it is looks large. The red and gold streaks of fresh paint remain shiny as they dry.

Heru tries to ask what the symbol is, but he's forgotten about the gag that Agatha so kindly gifted him with.

Bagatha must have psychic powers because she has little difficulty deciphering his muffled question. "It's a falcon," she answers his unintelligible question. Her zaffre-blue eyes dart around the space, searching for the other women before she leans in closer, paintbrush held a safe distance away now that her masterpiece is complete.

"You must remember. *Resut,* Herus," she urges, whispering close to his face. "The next stage . . . It is much worse than paintings. *Resut.*"

The linen cloth in Heru's mouth has grown damp and soft, collecting his saliva like a sponge. Even without the gag, he wouldn't know how to respond. How does one just force themself to remember what they've forgotten?

The urgency of her words spike fear in Heru, creating a sensation of spiders crawling up his spine. An instantaneous rush of anxiety in his chest.

Bagatha whispers one last, "*Resut,* Herus!" before pulling away and fussing with the nearby paints. The falcon painted on Heru's chest has dried in the span of their one-sided conversation, and the vermilion and maize arches and swoops have begun to itch.

Heru wants to scratch them. He wants to wash the paint from his feet and never let another soul touch them again. He wants to wake up in his garlic-scented apartment. Away from these strange women with their white robes, unfamiliar accents, and shiny, painted braids. Heru has accepted that this lucid dream will not involve orgies of any kind and as such, he'd very much like the dream to end now.

He closes his eyes against the warm glow of the torchlights. He ignores the voices of the women chattering in hushed tones in their odd language. Ignores the itching of the paint and the discomfort of the bindings. Ignores the way his back aches from laying on the stone altar. Heru sets his discomforts and displeasures aside and breathes.

A slow, even inhale. A long, deliberate exhale.

Another. And one more.

Heru opens his eyes, prepared for ugly tiles of his apartment ceiling. Prepared for the ever-present scent of garlic. Prepared to feel Cleo lying next to him. Prepared to hear Danny shuffling from their shared bathroom to the kitchen. Heru is prepared to leave behind this strange dream, these strange women.

Heru opens his eyes to find Agatha standing at the foot of the altar, holding a tool that appears to be a grotesque combination of a spork and a scalpel. The gleaming metal tool has a rounded head, caved inward as if meant to scoop. Instead of finishing with a curved, smooth edge though, the tool splits into tines with edges that shine sharp enough to slice stone.

Fuck.

Agatha is chanting in her unfamiliar language again. Bagatha and Lagatha's voices join hers. A chorus of beautiful women chanting.

In a different setting, they could be a choir worshipping their deity; in another, a cult proclaiming their obedience.

Heru catches, "*Resut*" thrown in their chant a few times, but the rest is indecipherable. The women could be wishing him well or condemning his soul, and he wouldn't know the difference.

Maybe, if they could just tell him what he's supposed to remember.

Bagatha and Lagatha are on either side of his altar now, words throaty and esoteric. In unison, they each grip his wrists just above the metal bindings that secure him to the altar. Agatha fists a hand in his hair from somewhere behind the altar that Heru cannot see.

Bagatha stares at him, a final plea evident in her eyes.

Resut, Heru! Bagatha's earlier words reverberate through his mind, a desperate appeal. An anguished prayer.

Agatha tips Heru's head back with a sharp tug, adding a sharp bend to the angle of his neck. Heru tries to shake off her grip but the stone altar and metal bindings are unforgiving. They allow no room for escape and no reprieve from Agatha's manhandling.

Awake, Herus!

All at once, the women fall silent. Their chant has ended.

Agatha lifts the devilish spork-scalpel in her free hand. Bagatha and Lagatha hold tight to Heru's arms. He writhes under their grip, immobilized but desperate. He can't get the fabric gag out of his mouth. Saliva runs over his chin and cheeks as he wiggles and thrashes, trying to dislodge the fabric. Trying to free himself. There's nothing good that can come from the instrument Agatha is holding.

She mutters in her strange language to Lagatha, and the other woman reaches up to replace Agatha's grip on his head. Lagatha's hand is stronger than Agatha's, and she pins his head down to the stone.

Heru wants to wake up. Wants it with a fearsome and overwhelming desperation he's never experienced. He doesn't want to continue this dream. Doesn't want to know how it ends.

WAKE UP!

He doesn't wake up.

Agatha's newly freed hand peels apart his left eyelid, holding his skin taut to keep his eyelid from closing.

Panic hits Heru like a tsunami, absent one moment and flooding his senses the next. His pulse skyrockets, chest thumping as if his heart might burst from his chest at any moment. His skin feels simultaneously frozen and overheated. The hieroglyphs on his hands, feet, and chest are surely in danger of sloughing off with his sweat.

If panic is a tsunami, the pain of Agatha's spork-scalpel tearing through the soft flesh of his conjunctiva is a wildfire. It starts slowly. Uncomfortable but almost unnoticeable with adrenaline fueling Heru's body. By the time he registers the pain, the sharp threat of the fire, it's far too late.

White-hot misery radiates from his left eye and cheek. Heru screams beneath his gag, jerking against his bonds. Tears stream from his right eye as his left suffers agonizing injustice. The last thing Heru feels before succumbing to the welcoming blanket of unconsciousness is a sickening *pop* from the location on his face where his left eye belongs.

U nconsciousness brings Heru ideas. *Dreams. Dreams within dreams.*

Heru sees himself, but altered. Different versions of himself—variations. Twenty-one variations.

One is wearing a white robe, like the female priestesses, praying to a god whose name he cannot speak. One stands above a city, overlooking his people, peaceful and prosperous. Another surveys a desert, vast empty space on all sides. Another version of Heru soars the skies, falcons at his back. One Heru watches over a dazzling twilight, ensuring the balance of day and night. A different Heru guides lineages of leaders, imparting wisdom and order.

Dozens of visions pass before him. Colors and swirls and variations of himself. Some younger, some older, some that carry the same vermilion and maize painted symbols, some with barren skin. The images flicker by Heru until they settle on a single scene. A singular Heru. No, not Heru.

The first Herus. Herus of the Horizon. Son of Osiris and Isis.

Herus of the Horizon is atop the very same altar that Heru is pinned to. The altar he now knows must be the center of the very temple dedicated to his worship. The first Herus stands tall and broad with the body of a man and the head of a falcon.

He turns his gaze on Heru. Herus of the Horizon has an eerily humanlike right eye. And his left . . . his left eye is milky white. Moonbeam white.

H eru wakes screaming.

His gag has been removed, but he's still bound to the stone altar in the room that he now knows is the center of the Temple of Herus, God of the Horizon.

Agatha, Lagatha, and Bagatha stare down at him warily. Agatha clucks her tongue at Lagatha and the other woman steps away from the altar. She returns with a mortar and pestle in hand. They're made of white stone with shimmering veins of gold.

She's twisting and grinding the contents. Heru is certain that he has no interest in learning the contents.

Bagatha peers down at him, concern and sympathy evident. "Did it work?" she asks.

Despite being free from his gag, Heru cannot respond. He cannot imagine how to respond. There's a dread-filled stone in his gut when a sharp pain returns to his face.

Sweat runs down his forehead, blurring his vision, but he's too afraid to move, even to blink.

"My . . . my eye. What did you—" Heru can't bear to finish. He can't bear to ask what's become of his left eye.

Bagatha winces, guilt and shame in her deep blue eyes. She pats his chest placatingly before responding, "It's almost over now. The hardest part is done."

Lagatha snorts, clinking the mortar and pestle nearby. She mutters under her breath and Bagatha retaliates with a sharp glare.

"Herus," Agatha begins, and Heru promptly flinches. He'd almost forgotten her presence in the quiet after the storm. She ignores his reaction and continues, "The final phase requires a willing participant. Do you understand?"

Heru doesn't but he nods.

Just let it end.

The women unfasten the bindings at his wrists and waist and Heru sits up, the altar solid beneath him. He notices that they don't release the bindings on his ankles. *Perhaps 'willing participant' has a flexible definition.*

Lagatha has added liquid to the concoction she's stirring and the mixture sloshes and gurgles as if almost sentient.

"You saw Herus, didn't you?" Bagatha asks, voice soft with wonder.

"Hush. It's time," Agatha snaps. Heru doesn't know what comes next. He doesn't *want* to know what comes next.

It's the mixture.

Of course, it's the mysterious contents that Lagatha has been quietly mixing this whole time. She presents the bowl to him carefully, and he peers down at the off-white contents. The mixture is something between liquid and gelatin.

Please taste like pudding.

Agatha grips his chin with tight fingers and forces him to meet her gaze. "You must finish it. Understand? All of it," she snaps.

Heru nods, taking the bowl from Lagatha. He takes a quick breath before lifting it to his lips.

It's not pudding. Thick, viscous liquid streams from the bowl to his mouth and then trickles down his waiting throat. It's warm, salty, and vile. Somehow tasting both gamey and slimy.

Heru gags, choking on the mixture. He starts to cough as Agatha and Lagatha start to chant. But now, the words sound familiar.

"Resut, Herus of the Horizon. Rise to claim your young form!
Awaken and bring balance that your power may transform!"

The mixture coats his throat and Heru coughs harder, heat blooming in his cheeks. He wants to stop drinking. He desperately wants to wake with no memory of this dream—of this pain. Wants to forget the Herus that came before.

But he can't put the stone bowl down. Can't pull it away until he's finished. He can't help but follow Agatha's orders. His fingers won't release their grasp, his lips won't close to deny the mixture entry. His body no longer answers his commands.

He continues sipping between racking coughs and gags. His stomach churns, a ship in a storm. Heru brings a paint-covered hand to his mouth, hoping to contain the acid building in his chest.

"I can't—It won't stay—" His words cut off, too afraid that if he opens his mouth again, he'll vomit.

Lagatha and Agatha are still chanting, voices bold and loud.

"*Resut, Herus of the Horizon. Rise to claim your young form! Awaken and bring balance that your power may transform!*"

But Bagatha—Bagatha stands at the end of the altar crying. Tears of liquid gold stream down her face, dripping off her chin to leave golden droplets on her white robe.

"Herus, I'm so sorry," she wails, reaching for his bound ankles. "Your eye—I never meant—"

There's a sharp *crack* of bone meeting stone and everything goes black.

Heru jolts up in bed, choking. He trips and tangles in his sheets in a mad dash to the bathroom. It isn't until he finishes gagging, knees sore against the unyielding bathroom tiles, that his setting rushes in. Heru has never been happier to smell garlic.

"Babe? Are you okay?" Cleo's voice calls from beyond the bathroom door. Heru's quick to flush the toilet, eager to spare his girlfriend the indignity of suffering his nightmare-induced vomit.

"Yeah. I'm fine. Just woke up feeling sick. You can go back to bed. I'll be right there," he responds quickly.

Heru peels himself off the bathroom floor and inspect his image in the mirror. Same face, same paint-free chest, same two eyes in his head where they belong.

After doing the best he can to clean himself up, Heru quietly returns to his bedroom. He eases the door open, aiming not to disturb Cleo if she's managed to fall back asleep while awaiting his return. Heru approaches the bed just in time to see Cleo frantically wiping liquid golden tears from below her zaffre-blue eyes.

Resut, Herus.

About the Author

EJ: Took a coma nap this afternoon and dreamt about this server lol. I woke up thinking "I have to ask the server this!" but I can't remember what I'm supposed to ask.

MDC: The answer is yes, we would LOVE to contribute to an anthology for you!

BB: I know I've been away but I caught wind of the anthology idea and I'M 100% HERE FOR IT!

CP: Haha I also support an anthology

———⬦———

A nd just like that, in May 2023, this book was conceived!

As the owner of EJL Editing, Emma Jane Lounsbury usually works behind the scenes, helping authors perfect their book babies. She has been working as a freelance professional editor since 2015 and running EJL Editing since 2022. Emma Jane lives in New York with her husband and their four dogs and six chickens. Her work hours are spent reading, and her free time is spent . . . you guessed it, reading. Though this anthology will serve as her writing and publishing debut, she hopes it will be the first of many.

Emma Jane wants to extend her gratitude to Brandee, Brig, Cass, Christian, Ciar, Kelly, Maile, and Nelle for their participation, creativity, sense of adventure, and stunning writing. This project wouldn't exist without your amazing stories!

An extra special thanks goes out to Ciar for her magic in turning a manuscript into a book.

Additionally, a big thank you to Luke for the beautiful cover and for his infinite patience.

Last but not least, Emma Jane wants to extend infinite gratitude to Maddi for having the bravery to slide into her DMs and all the way into a job. Her moral support, editing skills, organization, and responses to EJ's endless messages have been indescribably invaluable.

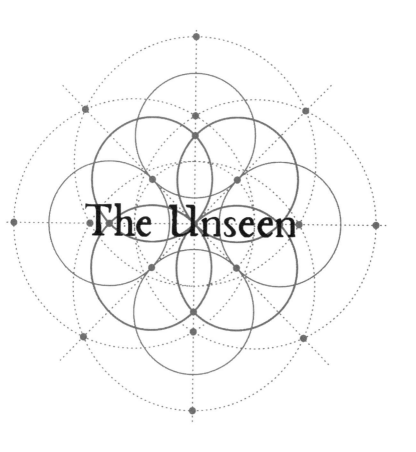

The Unseen

Snippets from an Unknown Realm

Ciar Pfeffer

Content/trigger warnings:

Violence, gore, manipulation,
implied sex, body mutilation

For people who like Squid Game, Hunger Games,
Black Mirror, The Twilight Zone

Representation:
Mental health/disability, BIPOC, LGBTQ+

Warning

The following text is the true account of one of our own.

Names have been redacted or
changed to protect those involved.

Proceed with caution.

Day One

Chapter One

T he smell of fresh paint saturated the air, turning Sally Joe's stomach. The stench of 'new' burned through her nose and made her limbs tremor. Some people loved smells like that, but she hated it. It aggravated her sinuses and upset her stomach to the point where she often vomited.

"You're being dramatic, oversensitive," her mother used to say. 'Used to' being the key phrase. Both of her parents died a long time ago, leaving her to her aunts who raised her with their kids. While it had been nicer than living with her biological parents, being unloved or semi-loved was all Sally had ever known.

She ran to the bathroom and threw up everything she had eaten that morning. The entire condominium reeked of new leather, carpets, hardwood finish, and much more. Most people would never complain about getting a bougie brand-new tenth floor apartment with an amazing view of the city, fabulous promotion and a paid relocation. But Sally, as grateful as she was, could have done with something less flashy.

And smelly.

After washing her face and brushing her teeth again, she fluffed out her long, dark, wavy curls that had fallen out of place when she ran into the bathroom. The deep browns in her hair highlighted her rosy cheekbones and pale white face beautifully. She smiled, grateful for the makeup lessons she had received from her oldest cousin.

However much it irritated her, her ability to see, sense, smell, and even feel everything to an extreme was how she got so good at her analyst job. And how she landed the new position. The three degrees she held in finance, business, and intelligence analytics solidified it for her. Learning had always come easy to her, whether in school or on the internet. She absorbed information so fast and retained all of it. Pushing her to the top of her class wherever she went and earned her several degrees in months.

The back of her throat itched and heaved as her stomach turned again. She walked around her new place, opening all of the windows, thankful for the cool spring air cleansing her place. It was crisp and fresh from the rain the night before. On her way home after work, she needed to stop and look for an air cleaner.

"TV on, news station 121."

The oversized television, that also came with the apartment, flickered to life and she finished getting ready. Jeans since it was Friday and a cute top under her short-sleeved cardigan, in case she matched with someone while at work. She preferred to be ready rather than run back home to change.

"Earlier this morning, after the rainfall washed away some of the nearby park, numerous skeletal remains were discovered. Nothing is known about the bones other than they are human and appeared to be from more than one person. Authorities are saying that these bones have been there for a very long time and give no reason to worry the populace. And now for the weather report." The weather reporter came on the screen as Sally walked back into the kitchen to make some tea.

Peppermint to soothe her stomach and chamomile to soothe her nerves. A weird combo but she enjoyed the flavor contrast. She grabbed a few snacks to compensate for hurling her breakfast and made a mental note to grab a big lunch later. And an early one. Slinging her bag over her shoulder, she looked around to make sure everything was off.

Coffee pot: check

Oven: check

Iron: check

Why do I always check the iron? I can't remember the last time I even used it. Sighing to herself, she locked the front door. The elevator got halfway down to the bottom floor before she remembered her TV. At least that could be turned off from her phone.

The air outside welcomed her and the refreshing air cleansed her stinging nostrils, freeing them from the smells in her apartment. Her building had fifteen floors, but it was the smallest building on the block. The city sprung to life around her as the sun continued to rise. Street lights were going off, people were leaving their buildings, and buses had already started picking people up.

It's only fifty feet.

It's only fifty feet.

It's only fifty feet.

She repeated that to herself every morning on her walk to the car. Her rendezvous with the toilet that morning had delayed her enough that now people were out and walking to their cars, jobs, and bus stops.

People suck. They only take what they want from you and never give back. Sally never liked anyone and only ever interacted with them when absolutely necessary. It wasn't only because of her upbringing and lack of love from her parents, but every person she had ever analyzed turned out to be exactly the same. Since Sally had never been able to separate her job skills from life skills, she always overanalyzed everything and everyone she ever met. Her aunts spent years trying to undo it with mild success. Well, enough to get Sally to try 'dating.'

Her aunts loved each other, a fairytale story. They wanted that for all of their children. *I guess that means me too.* If they knew she never actually dated, but had one-night stands, what might they think?

She liked sex but hated people. Thank the heavens they made apps for that. She frequented them often and had no shame about it. Thinking about her aunts caused her to sigh again. They had been calling her recently, asking her to come visit for the holiday coming up. But her new job had taken her hundreds of miles away from them and the idea of getting on a plane horrified her.

"Sally Joe!" The red-haired and freckled woman called from the sidewalk. When she didn't get an answer, she moved closer. "It's Sally Joe, right?"

The lady stood a few feet away from her, delicately framed like Sally, but shorter and less wide. As men told her all the time, she was curvy in all the ways anyone would want with gorgeous hips and luscious thighs.

"Yes, it is, Miss—" Sally tried to cut the woman off and continue on her way, but the lady had other plans.

"*Mrs.* Porter, but you can call me Joleen. I live below you; I believe we met when you moved in?"

"Possibly. I don't really remember. It was a busy day," Sally replied. She moved one of her feet, trying to signal she had to leave. Joleen ignored her.

"You were certainly rushing around. I offered to help, but you must not have heard me." The older woman pushed her glasses up her nose. *Older's a bit offensive.* Her attitude annoyed Sally but she couldn't have many years on her. Maybe mid to late thirties.

"Sorry. I typically wear earplugs," Sally said, removing one of them so she could see.

An unexpected knowing look washed over the woman's face. "Oh, I see. My oldest son uses them as well. It helps with over-stimulation." She took a few steps back, giving Sally some much needed space.

The recognition of Sally's needs and execution without bringing attention to it made her smile. It reminded her of her aunts. "Thank you. I really do need to get to work."

"Of course, have a lovely day," Joleen said, her lips curved up in a warm smile.

"You too," Sally replied.

Work passed by quickly, Sally had a report to present and three meetings regarding potential assets the CEO wanted to acquire for the company. Two of which Sally knew she had to break the news to him were not going to be worth the time or money. The boss appreciated her knack for detail, but she noticed he disliked how often it disagreed with what he wanted or had planned.

On the elevator, her phone dinged, a local match. She had to close all the news apps she had open to get to Hinder. During the day, she had read some news reports—a long-standing habit of hers—and more bones had been discovered due to a landslide from the heavy rain. *So strange*, she thought to herself.

When she finally got to the dating app screen, she closed her phone and rolled her eyes. The last several matches were men she had already hooked up with. Frowning, she walked out of the building to her car.

The wind tossed her hair around and the sky threatened open up at any time. *Great, more rain,* she thought. Her phone dinged again, and she smiled. *Damn, he's hot. And a new face. The things she would let him do to her—*

'Free tonight?' the message read. John Doe. His name sounded lame. And very drab. But his cheek bones, broad shoulders, and biceps sucked her in. He had dark brown skin, a goatee, and a bald head. She had always had a thing for men with bald heads and beards. Goatees were weird, but she didn't mind it on him. She kind of wanted to lick it.

'I am,' she replied. 'Want to come over?'

'Haha,' the message popped up, and the dots that indicated he was still typing followed. 'Right to business? I like that. But I just got off work. How about I treat you to dinner first?'

Sally gritted her teeth and stopped walking. She tilted side to side and then paced in a small circle. It's not that she didn't like going out to eat, she loved food. But the last few times she tried to have a meal or even a drink with one of her flings, it went south fast. He had no personality, though he made up for it in the bedroom, but dinner had been a drag.

She clicked on his profile and scrolled through it. He liked to hike, read, and go to the movies. Frequented the gym. Stuff like that. Not terrible.

'Alright, we can do that. Where were you thinking?' she asked. Despite asking, she mentally already had a list of places she preferred—ones that didn't over stimulate her.

'How about Richard's Diner over on Park Road? It's a local place, small farm-to-table. It's usually pretty quiet this time of day.' As she read the last message, her lips curved up. That was one of her favorite spots. It was on the outskirts of the city; the buildings were smaller and less populated. Perhaps the night wouldn't be so bad.

'Sounds good. I can be there in ten minutes,' she replied.

'See you then!'

Day One

Chapter Two

Dinner flew by and Sally couldn't remember the last time she spent so much time talking. They chatted all through dinner and then decided to walk along the pier. There was a new shop she wanted to check out there and he had suggested a stroll.

"What do you do for work?" John asked, reaching out for her hand. She allowed it, intertwining her hand into his.

She laughed, and he peered at her but couldn't hide his smile. "Is your job funny?"

"Normally, people start with that question, don't they? But you started with, what was it again?" she responded, holding back more laughs.

"What you had thought about the new action movie with Tim Cryse," he said, giving her hand a light squeeze.

"Yes that, never liked him."

"Me either."

They both laughed again.

"I analyze potential businesses that the company I work for wants to acquire or use in some way."

"That sounds really cool and difficult."

"It's a lot of reading and researching."

"That's your favorite part, I bet," he said with an ear-to-ear grin.

"Yea, it is," she replied with an equally big smile. "I love it! I have degrees in intelligence, data, and business analysis. I may even go back some day for financial analysis. But for now, I work with these."

"I bet you don't even need them or the degrees," John said with a slight chuckle.

Sally smiled again. He wasn't wrong. She had a photographic memory with near perfect analytic skills. Allowing her to read anyone around her, and for whatever reason always knew which direction north was, and by default east, west, and south. But she would never say that out loud.

The clouds had cleared, and the stars sparkled in the sky. It had rained while they were eating, and both were walking in zig zags, trying to avoid the puddles. A car drove by and nearly soaked Sally, but John stepped in front of her, taking the brunt of it. Her stomach swelled and her cheeks flushed. Had she gotten wet, the night would have been over. The sensation of clothes sticking to her skin made Sally want to curl up and quit all things.

"Thanks," Sally mumbled.

"No problem," he said, bringing his hand up to cup her face and gently tracing her cheek bone. His eyes met hers with a steady gaze and he continued, "You've been stepping over puddles and side stepping even the smaller ones."

The look on his face softened and she saw compassion take over.

"I would have gone home," she unexpectedly admitted.

A siren sounded in the distance and her hand twitched. Sally hadn't put her earplugs in because she wanted to be able to hear him without constantly asking him to repeat himself. The noise drowned out everything despite still being blocks away. Frantic, she looked around to see if there were any stores or places she could duck into.

Nothing.

They were still on the pier.

Her hands began to shake and her breathing shallowed. Without realizing, she lifted her right arm and began to scratch her left bicep and then grip it. Every second it got closer, her body reacted. Her bones felt like they were being electrified, and her mind raced. The sounds got louder and echoed from a distance. It wasn't just one truck, but several and they were speeding down the road.

Suddenly, the world went quiet, and her ears felt warm. She opened her eyes to see John looking down at her with a soft smile on his face. He had taken off a shirt, wrapped it around his hands, and covered her ears. In addition, he stood in front of her so she couldn't see the road when the truck passed by. He brought his face in a little bit closer and whispered, "I wasn't sure if it was the sound or lights that would bother you. I'm sorry for getting so close without permission."

A tear slid down Sally's face and he wiped it off with his thumb as she shook her head gently. She grabbed his head and pulled him in for a kiss as her heart exploded.

H ours later, the pair lay in her bed, naked and happy. Sex had always been fun and thrilling for Sally, but that time had been different. There had been an unfamiliar warmth. John lay next to her, grazing her arm and shoulder with his fingertips.

"We never got to go to that store, did we?" he asked.

"No, but I'm not complaining about the sidetracking," she said, scooting near him to kiss him briefly. She smiled, thinking back to the making out, breaking for a snack. Watching a movie, then switching to the bedroom. *What a night.*

He rolled on to his back and pulled her with him so that she curved into his body. Her arm draped over his unnecessarily ripped stomach. She knew he was fit from his photos, but she could never have imagined how defined his muscles were.

Normally, when they had finished, she sent them home. But she wanted to keep John there. For the first time *ever*, she wanted to see someone again. However, on her profile it said one night only, and she was afraid to ask.

"It's too bad there were no survivors," John said. A clear topic shift. Maybe he didn't want to see her again. She pulled in on herself a bit, tucking her arms near her chest. Oddly, he responded by pulling her closer.

"Yea, the number of trucks was insane. I don't think I've ever seen that many emergency vehicles going in the same direction. How do you think it happened?"

"Who knows, but I am never flying again. To think everyone on board liquified because the cabin didn't depressurize. But how did it reach that kind of pressure, anyway?"

"Maybe someone tampered with it," she said. He nodded, and she closed her eyes. Dying like that on a plane made no sense. It's not like it was a submarine underwater with a breeched hull. The plane landed and docked, but when the door opened, everyone inside died. A freak accident.

Like the bones.

Or the woman from the previous week that had been found in the street severed in half.

Or the young man that fell apart walking to work, with no blood in his body or anywhere.

Everyone around her accepted these things. She was starting to question them more and more. Especially since moving to her new location, the events had gotten weirder. Lately, she had started to wonder if the job was worth it and had been considering moving back to her old one.

"Can I stay until morning? I'm exhausted." He pulled her up to him for a kiss. "Someone wore me out."

"Sure," Sally said before she even had time to think about responding. *One night would be fine, right? John was different.* She wanted more of him, but didn't understand what that meant. Or why. He pulled her a little closer, kissed the top of her head, and her extremities tingled. Her heart raced and head felt light. But most of all, she felt safe.

Day Two

Chapter Three

The building exploded with sounds at five in the morning. Men and women ran through the halls, sirens blaring outside. Sally's body hurt to its core and her head pounded. She bit her lip to prevent herself from screaming, but it didn't work. She jolted up, clutching her head as she rocked back and forth.

Something stirred beside her and she panicked. Fear clutched her soul, and she tried to force her body to move. But she couldn't. The thing next to her got closer, but she refused to open her eyes until she felt it.

Warm hands over hers, and she realized he was whispering to her. It was John.

Obviously, it was John. Sally shook her head, ashamed she had forgotten he was there.

"Hey, hey," John whispered, "what do you need? Can you get to the bathroom? It might be quieter in there."

Her body violently shook at the thought of moving. She needed her headphones, but they were far away. In the night-stand. She needed to tell him but how. She pounded her head to make the sounds stop.

"Drawer," was the only thing she managed to say.

It took him a few seconds to realize what she meant and less time to grab them and get them on her head. After that, he sat with her until she calmed down. Once her heart and head grew silent and body stilled, he released her and said, "I want to make sure it's safe to be in the building."

She nodded, got up, and dressed. Waiting was not her strong suit, so after John left the apartment, she followed him downstairs. Why should he be the only one to see what had happened? But after she rounded the corner, she regretted it. On the ground, outside one of the doors, she saw a yellow flowered dress. Well pieces of it anyway, the same one Joleen had been wearing. But it was soaked in blood.

She shrieked and covered her mouth to cover the stench. Blood covered the floor, the walls, everything. But Joleen's limbs were blood free, as if every ounce of blood that had been in them had been drained. There had to be fifty perfectly cut pieces of Joleen. Her apartment door was open, and she heard someone say it must have happened when she opened her door. An interior pressure failure. Or an isolated bomb.

Nothing they said made sense, but everyone around them nodded. John ran up to Sally. He was talking to her, but she didn't hear anything except the screams that kept escaping her mouth. Her body was moving without her permission. John was dragging her back to her apartment. Back in her closed space, she finally heard the words he had been repeating.

"Sally, I need you to pack."

"What?"

"Sally, it's not safe here. They moved up Joleen's death, which means they probably moved yours up too." He paused to look out the window. "Shit, they're still here."

"Who's still here, John? You're not making any sense!"

"You're an analyst, right? Tell me what you saw in the hallway today and about the airport last night."

"They were freak accidents..." she didn't finish her sentence and the way he stared at her; he knew. She sighed, picking up her water to drink before continuing. "Technically, that don't make any sense or follow the actual laws of science, but I'm not a scientist, so what do I know!"

"That's because it *wasn't* in based science. I need you to pack."

"No. And what do you mean, not science based? So what then? Magic?" She scoffed at the idea. *That shit belonged in fairytales.* And she did not live in a fantasy realm.

"Sally, please, I don't have time to explain. But where you live is separate from the real world and divided—"

"What the fuck do you mean, separate *and* not real?"

"I don't have time to explain, but the short version is you're part a larger world where you are not in control of all of your actions."

Sally stared at him, but words failed her and after he gave her half a second to process that, he continued with what she hoped was bullshit.

"Where you live is partitioned into seven sectors, A through F, with a special bonus sector, Sector S. Where people from the outside pay to have things happen, for pleasure and amusement.

Will you please pack?" He looked outside one more time before reaching behind him to pull a gun from his belt.

"Where did that come from?" she asked, unable to process anything he had said. Focusing on what she could see and knew was the only thing keeping her grounded in that moment.

"My belt," he replied.

"No, you asshole! Have you had that with you the whole time?"

"Get down!" he shouted as the door burst open. Two men in masks entered but stopped when they saw John with the gun and looked at each other.

"What are you doing here, John?" one of them asked. They knew his name. They knew John. Men in her place were holding guns and John knew them.

"Leave. I don't want to hurt either one of you," he said.

"You know we can't do that. And you know we'll have to report you for this. They don't put up with this in Sector S. You know better!" the one on the left shouted. Before the other one could say anything, John fired his weapon twice. With extreme precision because both men fell to the ground before they knew what hit them.

Sally looked over at John, but her world started to spin and she dropped the water glass she was holding. Realizing far too late it had tasted weird. She felt John's arms catch her as she crashed toward the floor, almost positive he said he was sorry.

Well, fuck that.

"John, what the hell do you think you are doing? You brought a Sector S escapee here? Are you out of your mind?! They will never let her leave, you know that!" An unfamiliar voice was yelling at John, but Sally's mind spun around. Mist washed over her mind, clogging her thoughts. Unable to fully process anything.

Sector S.

John had said something about sectors last night. Before he had drugged her. Weirdly she had always wondered what that felt like. Not anymore.

Years of watching crime documentaries and taking science classes for fun told her that she hadn't been chloroformed. That took several minutes to take effect, and she went out in less than one. And she had drank it, not inhaled it. Ketamine was a good suspect. Not that what he had used mattered right then.

Her head felt like a ton of bricks and her body shook. Any movement made her want to puke and her already over sensitive nose was currently on fire.

Breathing hurt, but slowly she regained steady control. Without moving, she tried to open her eyes. Whoever was talking was not in the same room as her. The room was blurry, but small, with her on a small cot in the corner of it. She smelled dirt. A lot of it.

"She's going to wake up soon. Could you please not shout," John said. Sally tried to lay still. The voices were still in the other room, but moving might alert them.

"Is that why you're making soup, to say sorry for knocking her out?" the other man said.

"Bob," John said.

So his name was Bob.

"John," Bob replied with what Sally could only decipher as intense sarcasm. She held back a giggle. She hoped the impulse to laugh was a side effect of the drugs.

"I can't let her die," John said.

"Why? Because you fell for her? She's on their list and from Sector S! Come on!" Bob's voice had trailed off a bit. He must have walked to the other side of whatever room the two men were in.

He fell for me? That made her both happy and creeped out at the same time. *Nope. Cut the crap. Focus. Saving you or not, the man stole you, drugged you, and stored you in what must be an underground locker. Focus.*

"Not intentionally, and she was on the list before they moved her. It's not the first time we have followed someone into a different sector—"

What the hell? A list? What does any of this mean?

"No, but it *is* the first time from Sector S. S John, S!" Bob said, interrupting John.

What is so important about Sector S?

"We fly under the radar, remember? We get the ones out that we can. But when we started this, we knew it would never be all. It can never be all. They won't allow it. And they certainly will not let you waltz out of here with an Omega. They are far too rare," Bob said.

"We don't know that she's an Omega. As far as anyone knows, they are all but extinct," John said.

"Right, which is why they round up anyone like her and send them to Sector S. And once someone is in Sector S, you cannot take them out. The people who pay for Sector S put far too much money in it for one of their pets to go missing," Bob said as though he was scolding a child.

Moving sent daggers all through her entire body. Making her way to the door with no noise, damn near impossible. But she somehow had managed and when she spoke, they both jumped. "What's an Omega? And what do you mean save some but not all?"

She stood in the doorway of a room slightly larger than the one she had woken up in, with only one window at the top of the north wall. Definitely underground. They both stood there, looking at her wide eyed. Bob moved toward her, but John stepped in his way.

The room spun, and her world went dark. But not before she had the chance to puke.

Day Three

Chapter Four

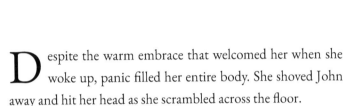

Despite the warm embrace that welcomed her when she woke up, panic filled her entire body. She shoved John away and hit her head as she scrambled across the floor.

"Sally, please wait," John begged.

Her vision blurred. Moving too fast always did that to her. Air entered her lungs but didn't leave and her head filled with more and more fog.

"Breathe with me, come on. Inhale: one two three four, okay now hold one two—"

Without realizing it, she started breathing in rhythm with his cues. At least now she understood why he was so good at calming her down. He had studied her and her— *What word had the men used?*—her kind. She scrunched her nose and swung her arm.

He caught it with ease and whispered, "You can beat me up all you want after I get you out of here. There's a table over there. Can I help you to it?"

She shook her head and shrugged off his help. The breathing had helped clear her vision and she could see the room now. It was a small bunker like building. Like? No, it was definitely a bunker. The kind you read about in conspiracy theory novels. *Great, John's a quack.*

"I know what this looks like, but at least hear me out?"

"Or you'll drug me again?" Sally snipped.

"No, I won't. Look, I'm sorry. You were getting agitated—"

"I was—" she paused to glare at him. He lowered his arms and his smile wavered. "I was what? Are you serious right now?"

"Are you telling me you weren't agitated?" He gently looked her in the eyes and held his gaze. The same way he had their first night together. He wanted her safe, that much she knew.

"You're infuriating," she said.

"I know," he said between laughs.

"So, the reason you knew about me and what to do, how to help me, is that because I was on a list?"

John winced. "It's not that simple." He looked over at her, raising his eyebrows and then shook his head. "Yes, but not because they told me to. Once I noticed how I felt, I learned more about people like you and how to help. I've never wanted to get someone out more than I have wanted to get you out of here."

"And here is where exactly?" she asked, dodging the how he felt part. Sally honestly couldn't decide if she needed to be freaked out or feel special. It was a weird juxtaposition. And the fact she leaned more towards special needed to be dealt with. At some point.

"Right now, we are in Sector A in a safe house. And, just so you know, I never would have made a move if you hadn't shown interest. The matching thing was accidental and not how I planned to meet up with you," he said, ignoring the fact she had ignored it. She rolled her eyes, and he sighed. "Do you remember what I told you the other night?"

"You mean before you drugged me?" she asked.

"You're never going to let that go, are you?" he said, and a smile cracked his lips. His eyes softened and somehow his presence around her grew tenderer.

"No, I'm not," she responded, returning the smile.

"I'm sorry," he said.

"Not good enough, but you can try to make it up to me later. But for now, explain."

"In addition to what I told you the other night—"

"Stop, start from the beginning. Everything you said was amidst gunfire and my neighbor being dismembered. My brain needs a fresh slate." Sally crossed her arms and sat back in the chair as she interrupted him.

"Fair enough. You live in an area that is controlled, unbeknownst to its inhabitants, by the outside world. There are primarily eight sectors, A through G, with a special Sector S. There are more, but most people don't pay for anything in the lower sectors because the effects are minimal. Each sector is designed to appeal to certain socio-economic groups, but it turned out that the less money people have the less interested they were in controlling people." He stopped there, taking a moment to look Sally up and down. He reached out to her, but she shrugged him away.

"Continue, don't worry about me keeping up. I watch documentaries for fun and listen to pod casts while I work," she said, shifting forward to lean her elbows on her knees.

"Right, so as the sectors grow in size, so does the amount of money required to make things happen."

"What kinds of things?" she asked, unsure she wanted the answer.

"In Sectors A through G, anything from minor inconveniences to miraculously surviving an accident: job loss, spousal abuse, cheating and honestly, anything you can think of people have paid to see it happen. It's broadcast at various times, much like a television show. Privacy is given to in home situations and only the things paid for are shown."

"That's disgusting but doesn't explain—" she paused, thinking about the skeleton remains, or Joleen, or the plane. "It doesn't—" she couldn't form a complete sentence. The thought alone tightened all of her muscles and filled her eyes with tears.

She sighed and her head plopped into her hands. No amount of rubbing her temples or massaging her scalp could make the crazy go away. Everything he said made no sense, but he wasn't lying. Her gut told her he was telling the truth. She had never understood all the weird things that kept happening. Where she used to live, they were small. But in Sector S, the plane, Joleen, the man on the sidewalk. All of it suddenly seemed to make sense.

"So people pay to see things happen in each sector, with what they can pay for increasing by price and space. And I was in Sector S?" She looked up at him, worried her need to repeat things might have annoyed him. But his gaze remained warm and sad. A small smile pierced his lips, and he lifted his hand again, stopping halfway. She closed the distance and intertwined her hand with his. He squeezed it before going on.

"Yes, it's the eighth sector that very few know about, only the super-rich," John said, like she knew what that meant. "People with more money than god, assuming god had money of course. Basically they can do whatever they want, run the world, and pay for whoever they want dead to be killed. Sector S is different because it usually brings people in from the outside world. Rarely does it bring in people from the lower sectors."

"Unless they think you're an Omega?" Sally asked.

"Heh, you heard that did you? Omega is another term for Shifters. Some parts of the world call them that, others Vessels. And I am sure that there are other names. But loosely, it means those that can see and sometimes use magic."

"Magic?" Sally laughed. There that word was again. John said it so easily. "Don't be ridiculous, all the magic in this world is gone. They drained it long ago." She shut her mouth then. Shocked at her own words. *How do I know that? Maybe I calculated it at some point and didn't realize it?*

"The very fact that you know that, analyzed it, figured it out, is why they want you dead. And in Sector S the deaths there are absolutely horrifying. They defy nature because—" he paused to look at her and he closed his eyes.

She remembered Joleen's dismembered body. The human soup that was left of the plane accident. And so many other things she had noticed. "Because they are for entertainment and unnatural."

"Yes."

"That's disgusting. I might puke again," Sally said, and she meant it. Her insides were churning. Humans were awful. *People really do suck.*

"A group of us have been trying to get people out, but we have never gotten an Omega out. They can see the old ley lines, or so they say. And if they can find the ley lines, they can bring magic back for everyone else, not only those misusing it in power."

"And why would anyone want to bring magic back?"

"To stop them, they're using magic."

"Who the fuck is they?"

"Sorry, the Government of the Treatied Territories. The old continent of Europe."

Sally's eyes went wide as she realized she didn't even know what that meant.

"And you? How are you involved?"

He winced, bringing his hand to his head. He rubbed the top of it before sliding it down his face. "I work for the Monitors. We keep track of the payments, what is supposed to happen, and when, often making it happen ourselves."

She glared at him, and he looked away before continuing, "Several years ago I started to question my job and I found out about a group of rebels. They work to get as many people as they can out of the sectors. And I've been with them ever since. We can't save everyone, but at least we can get some out."

Sally scoffed. *Some.* She doubted some would ever make up for all the crap that people had handed to them in the sectors for the sake of entertainment.

"I'll explain that more later, back to the magic, okay? They didn't just steal it, they sealed it off in a way that only they could access. Other parts of the world still use it. But we don't have enough time to get into anything else. Do you trust me?"

"I really don't love that my answer to that is yes, because it should be no. But here we are," she mocked. "I should make you take me home."

John's eyebrows came together and his face contorted. He looked at her then got up, walking over to what looked to be a cabinet.

She watched him clench his fists and open them a few times before he spoke. "If you really want to go home, I'll take you. But don't ask me to stay. I won't watch you die."

"Well, that's pretty fucking selfish," she said. "And manipulative."

He whirled around, his face taut. "I'm okay with that, if it keeps you alive."

"Look, I don't know if what you're telling me is true or not, but I'm pretty good at knowing when someone is lying. And you don't seem to be lying. So, for now, I'll trust you. But I don't trust Bob."

"I do, I've known him a long time. He'll help, we've been getting people out of the sectors for years. We never take out Omegas, because they are too risky. But, well—"

"Now there's me," Sally said. "Alright, let's leave. But from now on, run things by me first, okay? Try to remember calculating is my specialty. At least let me figure out the odds before we try anything."

"Alright, I can agree to that. How long does it usually take?"

"Less than five minutes," Sally said smiling.

"So what do you do at work all day?"

"Honestly, not much. I pretend it takes me all day," she said laughing. They both laughed. He moved closer to her, but she held a hand up. She wasn't ready. Not yet. She wanted to resume what they had started, but not until she was safe.

Considering what happened at her building, he wasn't completely lying, if he was even lying at all. Some people had absolutely tried to kill her. The ceiling shook, and some dust fell to the ground as a vehicle of some sort drove over them.

"I'll be right back, I want to make sure that's Bob. Come here," he extended his hand, and she took it. "I know you don't like tight spaces but can you manage in here for a few?" he asked her as he opened the door to a very small closet. The back of which opened into a secret, smaller space, for her to hide. Her voice was stuck in her throat and she gripped his hand. But she nodded. He pulled her in for a hug, kissed her on the forehead, and pushed her inside since she couldn't make her own feet move.

Day Three

Chapter Five

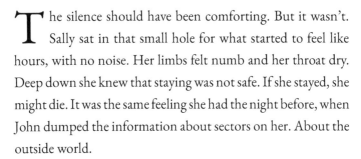

T he silence should have been comforting. But it wasn't. Sally sat in that small hole for what started to feel like hours, with no noise. Her limbs felt numb and her throat dry. Deep down she knew that staying was not safe. If she stayed, she might die. It was the same feeling she had the night before, when John dumped the information about sectors on her. About the outside world.

She took several long breaths and forced her body to move. She willed it.

Move.

Move.

Move.

The door creaked as she pushed it open, her nose picked up smells that weren't there earlier. Smoke. Not smoke from a fire, but almost metallic. And sulfur. Guns? *John! Where is John?*

She pounded her fist into her right leg, trying to calm herself all while forcing her body to move.

Get to the ladder.

Go outside.

No one was in the bunker and silence filled the air.

Go outside. You have too. Move!

The air around her felt heavy, and she took one last deep breath before she exited the bunker. Gun smoke and other gases filled the air. She held her hand over her mouth to silence her coughing.

A man lay still on the ground, and she froze. She didn't want to look but knew she had too. *What if it's John? Then what?* Her heart pounded so loudly her brain hurt from the sound. Before she had the chance to turn him over, she heard coughing.

"Sally? Sally is that you? I'm over here," John whimpered, his voice low and dry.

Relief fell over her but not enough to calm her nerves. She was still shaking when she reached him when the smell of blood washed over her and she had to stop herself from retching. Damn her nose.

"I'm okay, it's okay," John said.

"No, you're not. You're bleeding!"

"I didn't say I wasn't injured, I said I was okay. Which is true. Come here and help me up. We need to get into the truck and out of here. Can you drive?"

"Of course I can," she replied. She pulled his arm over her shoulder and struggled to stand. Eventually, she got John up and helped him to the truck.

Once the smoke cleared, she noticed that he had used a shirt to stop the bleeding. *What is with him and shirts, is it his only tool?* She stifled a laugh and rolled her eyes. "Do you have any gauze or bandages anywhere?"

"In the cab, back seat," he said as he leaned against the truck bed.

She searched under the seats until she found a large red box and started to clean and cover the wounds. He had a gash on his side and a few small cuts on his arms. Thankfully, Bob must have gone after him with a knife and nothing more.

"I'm sorry I left you down there. Bob came back. But only to get me. He said he had leaked this location. He wanted me to get out of here and leave you. But, I couldn't. I really couldn't."

Sally looked around, noticing dents in the truck, scuff marks on the ground. Blood splattered all over. He had fought for her. Whatever world she lived in, she wanted out of it. And he knew how to. She threw her arms around him, and he pulled her close. "Take me away from here."

"That was the plan all along. Now seriously, can you drive a standard?"

"I'll figure it out, I've watched videos on it," she replied.

"Of course you did," he smirked. The smile on his face melted her heart.

It took her some time, but she managed to get the truck moving and on the road in the direction that John wanted. They drove for hours and hours, going through each sector slowly until they finally settled in Sector D. Far enough from Sector S that they wouldn't be looking there just yet for them. Or so John said and she hoped.

"I have some contacts here, I'll reach out to them and see if they can get us anywhere."

Sally reached out and grabbed his hand, squeezing it. His wounds were still fresh, and although they had stopped to re-bandage them, he needed rest.

"What if—what if they do the same thing Bob did?"

"This one owes me a favor, I saved his daughter. It's how he got into this," John said. "And this time I won't tell them who you are and if we're lucky, they won't have notified this sector yet. Normally we hand people off where the sectors meet. But I know how to get through them and I've never told anyone. A secret I've never been happier that I kept."

"Alright, I'll wait here."

"Take this," he said handing her a gun. He took her hand in his and stood behind her. "Aim with both eyes, use the little knob at the top to aim."

"You mean the sight?"

"Yes. Let me guess, videos?"

"Yea, but that doesn't mean I'm not scared," she said. He leaned down and into her, pulling her up to him at the same time. His mouth met hers and she returned the kiss.

"I'm getting you out of here," he whispered into her mouth.

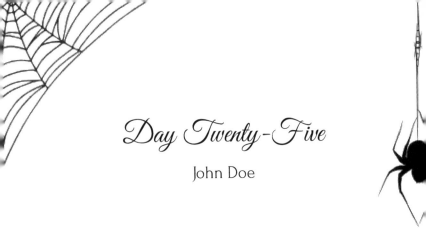

Day Twenty-Five

John Doe

John rolled over as he woke up, pulling Sally toward him. It had been nearly two weeks since he met her and had taken over ten days of hiding before his buddy had come through. She stirred next to him and he smiled. The sleeping headphones he had given her came with a cover for her eyes. According to her, she had never slept better.

He kissed her on the forehead and squeezed her one more time. Now that they were settled, he wanted to get back into his daily runs. His friend had really out done himself and found them a quiet town.

They needed to stay there for a few months before he contacted anyone, to ensure no one knew where they were hiding. He had kept the fact she might be an Omega a secret. But now that they were in the outside world, where the rebels were, he would need to look into it.

The morning smelled like fresh dew and his feet grew wetter and wetter as he ran up the trail. But he didn't care. The sun was shining and he had saved Sally. Nothing else mattered.

For the last several days John had run as far as he could, all in different directions. And always in areas he wasn't supposed too. A habit he had from being on the run and getting people out of the sectors. He smiled as he finished his run, climbing to the top of the trail. The view went for miles and miles. The town sat below, waiting for the sun to say hello. Most of the town was probably still asleep. The Monitors were likely looking for him. And his buddies who had helped him get to where they were now could only sidetrack them for so long without implicating themselves.

John turned around to leave but something caught his attention on the side of the mountain. The rock under his hands felt weirdly light, less dense as he moved closer to the writing. It felt hollow. John held his breath as he brushed aside the vines only to rush to put them back, covering the lettering he had exposed. He shimmied back to the ridge and dropped to his knees. He looked around and then started his run back down the mountain, forcing himself to breathe.

The faded writing had read 'Sector I.'

About the Author

C iar Pfeffer is a lifelong gamer, avid reader, and full-time day dreamer. She has been writing and rewriting stories for longer than she can remember. Currently, she lives with her two children and pupper in New England. Her debut novel, *Fractured...are the pieces*, is a NA fantasy with low, fade to black spice, some profanity, and mild violence. Experience mythical creatures in ways you never have before featuring a diverse cast, slow burn romance, forced proximity, a unique magic system, found family, engaging action scenes, and much more! When Ciar isn't writing, having fun with her children, playing Breath of the Wild, Kingdom Hearts, or board games, she works in the local school system.

Thank you for reading this short story and someday Ciar plans to return to this world. For now, check out the Fractured Realm, with book two coming early 2024!

Connect with her on social media:
Instagram — @ciar.pfeffer_author
Tiktok — @ciar_pfeffer

Website — www.ciarpfeffer.com

Widowed Crown

Christian Carter

Content/trigger warnings:

Death, violence, gore,
mentions of torture

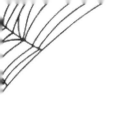

Chapter One

White smoke from Obi's pipe danced with the embers from the campfire in front of us. He was a strange man; one with many stories but was hesitant to share truths. I still valued his company, of course, and I didn't want the truth, anyway. His stories were the best escape from the dim reality ahead of me.

Obi let out another long exhale of smoke. "Colette," he whispered, his voice blending with the soft rain. "What did we say about bringing troubles to tea time?"

I snorted and replied, "To not bring them with me. After all, bad feelings ruin the taste of good tea." I leaned back on my hands, gloves protecting me from the jagged bark of the fallen log we had procured as a bench. Now free from the hood of my cloak, I let my red hair fall freely behind me as I tilted my head back. It only let me see more of the dark sky peeking into our shelter. It was a shame that the sun wasn't out today.

Looking every bit the sage with his large pipe and trimmed beard, Obi nodded and hummed a noncommittal noise of agreement. He kept his gaze locked firmly in the distance; through the rain and brush and the gnarled wood that made up the twisted trees surrounding us.

The playful smugness was well hidden, but I saw it in the twitch of the corners of his mouth. Coyly, I asked, "And what did I say about smoking that thing at tea time? That is going to kill you one day."

He coughed, interrupting his inhale of sweet-scented tobacco, and chuckled. Obi replied, "Ah, but death is simply the final journey that we all take , my young friend. Now, how about we actually have some tea so you can tell me what is troubling you?"

The tea pot resting on a stand above the burgeoning fire was outdated. Cracked, but not broken, with the appearance of something that was important long ago. I imagine it being used in tea ceremonies long ago or to serve royalty. The caricature of a young man wielding a sword in one hand and a woman's severed head in the other stood out starkly against the ornate black and gold pattern on the teapot and it seemed like a good topic as any to avoid my troubles with.

Another puff of smoke passed by my face as I set about pouring the tea into a set of chipped mugs. Rolling my eyes at Obi's attempts to sneak a huff of tobacco, I gestured to the teapot's imagery and said, "Let's have a story before we get to my mess. You've never talked about the man on your tea set. What's his story?"

Obi clicked his tongue before replying, "A story not so dissimilar to your own, Colette. Maybe a touch more dramatic, but still relatable to what I'm assuming your troubles are."

The ancient man leaned forward and tapped the tip of his pipe to the woman's head. He began, "This is Medusa. A monster in Greece with snakes for hair and the ability to turn men to stone with a gaze. Intelligent, and hateful toward the gods, she was a force to be reckoned with."

"The man holding her head is Perseus, son of the King of the Gods, Zeus. He killed her to prove himself to his father. This was just one of the many of his heroic deeds. He is one of the most renowned and accomplished heroes in all of Greek mythology."

I picked up my tea and passed the spare cup to Obi. A groan of satisfaction escaped me after my first sip. The warmth of the tea settling in my chest chased the remnants of cold from my bones. I took two more sips before I asked, "And how does that relate to what you assume my issue is?"

"Well," Obi replied after taking a sip of his own, "from our past conversations, I know you want to impress your father. From your mood lately, I'm assuming he asked you to do something that you would very much like to avoid doing. He has presented you with a Medusa of your own and he expects you to slay it."

We were quiet for a few minutes. I drained my cup and poured another. The rain was light enough now where I could see the surrounding forest. I like to imagine the trees as people in the town market; crowded, clambering over one another for space. It was better than seeing them as dark and crooked, fighting for space and survival.

Obi cut through the silence, his tone terse and tense. "Perseus still died."

"What?" I replied, bewildered. "How is that relevant?"

"Perseus received the approval of his father and his people. He was killed, taken too young."

"So, if I do what my father wants, then I die? How is this connected at all?"

"Tell me your dilemma, Colette, and then I will offer you an explanation. If you will listen."

So, I told him. I told him how my father didn't see my worth as a person, but only as a hand to be married off. I told him how I was being put through suitors and being bid on like an animal. I told him how I had until the month's end to decide between two men or else the decision would be made for me.

By the end of my rant, I was pacing in the drizzle, kicking up mud and flailing my arms. "I want to see the world, Obi!" I cried. "I want to meet people like you everywhere. Ones with stories and experiences. Anything outside of this small, nothing life I live."

I was glad Obi was my friend, but if he continued to give me monosyllabic, sage-like responses, I was going to snap. After a rather thoughtful, "Mhm," Obi was content to let silence stretch out indefinitely. It seemed to spread to the surrounding forest; the rain faded to the lightest of drizzles, crows restlessly shifted on their perches but remained silent.

Obi stood using the assistance of his gnarled walking stick. Standing slightly taller than the hunched form of my friend, it looked even older than the tea set, and it had never left his side in the year that I had known him.

Without a word, Obi took slow but confident steps out from their cover and into their small clearing. I hurried to put out the fire, calling after him, and grabbing my things before he disappeared into the crowded foliage.

I caught up with him a minute or so later, cursing under my breath about a gnarled root that caught my shin. Obi was always unnaturally calm in the forest. He stepped over roots without looking at the ground, avoided the abundance of sharp thorns with his gaze fixed forward, and never had unlucky encounters with the forest creatures like I do.

Obi continued his relentless march to the rhythm of me getting caught in the crush and knocked against low-hanging branches. He called back to me, "Do you remember what I told you about my wife, Colette?"

"Yes, I re—Ow!" I exclaimed as one of the aforementioned ravens decided to swipe me with its wing during its transition between trees. I replied while glaring at the feathered monster, "Yes, you speak of her often. Tati was very important to you."

"She is important to me, yes," Obi lamented. "Without her here, I feel like the world has lost color. It is like I am in a rainstorm, and the sun is never coming to break apart the clouds."

"And you remind me so much of her. The best and the worst parts of her all at once. It really can be quite unnerving, if I'm being honest."

My friend continued before I could interrupt him, "You both see the light in the world. Always. It is encouraging to see people so obsessed with the good that can be found in the littlest parts of life."

"But when something bad or strange comes your way." Obi tutted as if he were discussing some unruly children. "You are blinded and consumed by it. Confused and angry to the very end. Emotions like that make you rash, Colette, and you are not in a position where you can afford to make decisions hastily."

Obi was kind about it, as he always is, but it still hurt to be reminded that I was powerless. A dove, trapped in a cage, ready to be shot down if it escaped against its master's will.

"Now, Colette, no need to brood back there." Obi looked over his shoulder and smirked at me. I shuffled to a stop next to him, shivering slightly at the unfamiliar expression on his face. He raised his walking stick to point to a ruined stone structure resting atop a small hill.

"After all, Colette," Obi said, his smirk growing every second, "Your position can change with the right influence. And I have just the friend to help you."

Chapter Two

T he stone mass in the distance became clearer each time I was able to catch a glimpse of it through the crowded forest. There were no paths here; just tripping hazards and an ever-increasing number of crows. Their beady eyes followed me as if expecting me to drop dead.

Obi stopped following me about an hour ago. He said that the difficult terrain didn't agree with him. His friend would be waiting in the Court for as long as it took me to get there. The Court being the random building that was built on the highest hill in the most treacherous part of the woods.

The rain picked up again after a few minutes into my lonely hike. The heavy branches, usually only good for blocking sunlight, created some shelter from a good portion of the downpour as well. The ground was still slick with mud and my cloak was still drenched, but I appreciated the small blessing for what it was.

I reached the Court without much fanfare a half hour later. I was celebrating the rain finally stopped when one moment, I was ducking a branch, and the next I was stumbling into a clearing looking up, and up, and *up* at the towering pillars around me.

The structure was a long piece of flat ground surrounded on all sides by columns. Standing beneath them, for a moment, I wondered if they were supporting the sky to keep it from crashing down on us. There was no roof or any evidence of a roof ever existing.

Leaves and twigs crunched beneath my feet and I slowly slipped between two pillars to shuffle into the courtyard proper. The structure that I originally thought was made of stone was overrun with plant life; Ivy wound tight around columns, vines snaking around the various stone benches and chairs, gorgeous flower bushes catching my eye everywhere I looked. Even the floor, which I assumed would be solid, was an organic mix of cracked stone tiles with patches of lush grass peeking through the gaps.

It was about the size of the old church in the village, but much grander. It was . . . regal, in a word. Regal, yet wild. When I saw the two tall-backed chairs, it was impossible not to imagine a king and queen sitting on them. Rulers of the wilds that let the elements do what it wished to their domain.

"You know, Colette, you aren't far off at all."

A shriek leaped from my throat as I whirled around to see Obi lounging on one of the benches. My foot caught on a broken tile. I fell loudly on my backside, hissing when the stone shards cut my hand as I tried to catch myself.

Obi, looking perfect next to my well-worn and disheveled self, strode over to me with his walking stick leaning against his resting place. He put his hands on his knees and spoke through a smile. "My dear, I'm flattered. It's been many years since I have been able to make a beautiful lady such as yourself weak in the knees."

I snarled at him, which only prompted a hearty laugh, and he said, "Just a bit of fun, my friend. Let me help you with that."

Obi grabbed my bleeding hand and held it tightly between his palms. I went to shout in pain, but the sound died in my throat when our hands began to glow. My eyes snapped between our hands and my friend's face. Then I noticed the changes.

Even leaning down like he was, Obi stood taller and firmer than he ever had before. His face, forehead slightly crinkled, had somehow lost the age spots and wrinkles. The gray hair I was familiar with was now a shining silver, and his skin almost glowed instead of having the appearance of dried leather.

His features sharpened. The ruined cloak and patched pants melted away and in their place were a dark green waistcoat and brown trousers. Within seconds, the ancient hermit I knew had become the most handsome man I had ever met.

"There you go, my dear. Good as new!" Even his voice was smooth. Simple words flowed over me like a refreshing stream.

Obi let go of my hand and the wound was gone. Looking closer, even the little knife scar I've had for over a decade had completely faded away, only showing smooth skin. Perfect now where there was imperfection before.

My jaw sat unhinged at the man before me as he stood, a good six feet tall at his full height, and let his set of shining, translucent wings unfurl behind him.

"Ah, finally!" Obi said with a sign of relief. "It has been too long since I let my wings stretch out. I hope you don't mind them, Colette."

I made what must have been registered as a sound of approval as my friend smiled at me, teeth as white as snow, and said, "Well then, it seems actual introductions are in order. Allow me to introduce myself to you using my full title."

"You know me as your friend, Obi. We are still friends, of course, but feel free to call me by my true name."

Obi backed away with a flourish and bowed deep, arms stretched out on either side of him. He dipped his head once and then luridly pulled it back up to lock eyes with me for the first time since his transformation. They were a shimmering green color.

"My name is Oberon. King of the Fae, Father of the Seasons, and God of the Wilds. Colette, it is a pleasure to finally make your acquaintance as my true self."

I was frozen; unable to form words. Obi—*Oberon*—laughed and approached me again, holding out a hand. My own hand shook as I accepted his offering of a handshake. His skin was warm like the first ray of sunshine after winter.

His demeanor was pleasant, his words were kind. So different, yet so similar to the friend I knew.

Even with that familiarity, I couldn't deny the dread forming in my chest that formed when I saw the look in his eyes.

When I was a little girl, I saw a wolf on the outskirts of town. I was bringing back some berries from the forest's edge. I locked eyes with it as I was turning to leave.

It was sitting in the tree line. Spine curled, preparing to pounce, teeth poking out of its lower lip. Sharp eyes tracked my every move. I froze and dropped my berry basket as I turned to run.

It was on me in an instant. It ripped a chunk of flesh from my leg and sent me sprawling on the ground. I fought and punched and kicked as claws and fangs broke the skin on my arms and face.

My father was there in less than half a minute. He swung an axe into the beast's side, knocking it off me before swinging again to kill it on the ground.

I was covered in blood, both my own and the wolf's, and my wounds were burning as my father squeezed me tight. My wounds burned and blood clouded my vision. After I was cleaned up and bandaged, I didn't speak or eat for the day or so.

All I could see then and for many nights after was the image of a predator's eyes sizing up its prey.

The wolf's eyes were green and hungry, just like the man's eyes before me.

"Colette? My friend, are you alright?"

I shook myself out of my stupor as I kept pace with Obi—Oberon—my companion. I replied in the strongest voice I could muster, "Y-Yes, of course! Thank you for wondering, Obi. Oberon. Your Majesty?"

The king's booming laugh echoed around the Court. I stifled a flinch as he set a hand on my shoulder and said, "Colette, nothing has changed. You may call me Obi or Oberon, as I have not gone by 'Your Majesty' in a very long time. Especially not among friends."

"I'm sorry this is just a bit much. I—I don't know how you want me to respond."

I took a hesitant step back as a small knot of betrayal formed in my chest. My thoughts slipped out as words before I could stop them. "You reveal this to me after a whole year? Are we really friends?"

Oberon nodded, his brown hair shifting slightly from the motion. The dark strands stood out starkly against his fair skin. "Well," he replied, "I always meet my new friends in disguise. After a few meetings, I knew that our friendship was genuine, but . . . you took so much comfort from Obi. He was a welcome escape from your life and the expectations that came with it. Am I wrong?"

I bit my lip and stuttered back to him, "Well, no. But that doesn't mean that I wouldn't have been fine with knowing this either. You lied to me for months."

He let out a short *hmm* at my complaint. His eyes met mine, still similar enough to the wolf's eyes to make me shiver, and he said, "I know that was wrong now. Being a king doesn't make me perfect and I do hope you won't hold that against me, Colette. I'll make sure that I am honest with you in the future."

"I'll keep that in mind . . . Oberon."

Oberon smiled back, lips tight, and he gestured to the Court around him. Spinning in a circle with his arms open wide, he said, "Welcome to my Court! It has changed location and appearance many times throughout the ages, but it is always home to me. And now to you as well."

This was something I could talk about. It was hard to will the air up my throat and out as words. I replied, "It is beautiful in a wild sort of way. Like something out of a storybook."

"I'm glad you think so! My other friends throughout history have written about it, so technically it is something out of a storybook. Personally, I've always been a fan of Edmund and William's work. They did an excellent job at capturing some of mine and Titania's personalities, but still managed to spin a unique tale of their own creation."

I ignored the storybook comment in favor of asking, "Titania? Is that . . . ?"

Oberon's skin lost its glow as he frowned. His wings drooped behind him as replied, "Yes, that would be my wife, Tati, that I often told you about. Everything I told you about her was true. She has been gone for many years now."

Oberon took a moment to take a lap of his Court. I stood in the center of the room and watched him. He took his time. Oberon lovingly stroked the benches and chairs. He leaned on pillars and dragged his feet along the tiles. It reminded me of watching a blind man use his body to connect with the world around himself.

He cut through the comfortable silence with a terse voice. "It's true that she's gone."

I stepped toward him for the first time since his revelation. I kept my hands to myself, palms to my chest, trapping the remnants of my discomfort so I could speak to him. "Obi," I began, "I truly am sorry that she's gone. I don't know how to feel about all this magic nonsense you've revealed to me, but I know she meant the world to you, regardless."

Obi snorted. "Magic nonsense? I heal your wound and sprout wings, and you think it's nonsense?"

The familiar banter loosened the knot that had formed in my chest. I shot back with as much snark as I could muster, "A man of your age has to know a few tricks. You'll need to show me a little more before I believe you can do magic. Right now, you just look like a fancy street performer."

His laugh was more of a wheeze this time. He didn't reply with words, but instead gestured for me to follow him. At ease after the friendly exchange, I obliged.

We walked to the edge of the Court. All that was in front of us were a few dozen feet of bare dirt and miles of dark oak trees fighting for space. Thunderclouds still drifted across the sky, ready to unleash watery hell on the forest below.

Obi raised a hand to his mouth and let out a shrill whistle. A short few seconds later, a small fairy zipped out of the trees and stopped a few feet away from me.

Hovering in the air, at maybe three feet tall, was a wiry creature. He was . . . odd compared to the Fairy King. Not grotesque by any means, but he lacked the air of perfection that Oberon exuded as his true self.

His skin was a deep maroon, and he had small horns poking through his brown, wind-tousled hair. His dark wings let out a soft buzz as he floated in front of us. It was like listening to a hummingbird with a three-foot wingspan.

His left arm was missing from the shoulder down. The sleeveless tunic did nothing to hide the mass of scar tissue spread out over his shoulder joint and along the side of his torso.

"This is my old friend, Robin," Obi said. He pulled the smaller fairy in close to him and wrapped an arm around his floating friend's shoulders. "He is going to be serving us tonight. Come, it's time to eat."

"Uh, Obi," I interjected, "It's almost nightfall. I have to go home and I'm already nervous enough traveling through the woods in the dark."

Oberon looked back at me and rolled his eyes. He flicked his wrist and snapped his fingers with a flourish. The trees parted to reveal a tidy path leading to a homely dwelling only a few dozen yards into the forest proper.

The king began to walk down the path. He called out over his shoulder, "I thought you wanted help to escape your problems, Colette."

I did a double take at the casual display of what could only be magic. The trees started to close behind Obi. I found myself hurrying to catch him before my mind could process my actions.

I caught up with him quickly and fell in step beside him. Oberon walked briskly with obvious purpose. Heel toe, heel toe, almost like someone marching. His eyes were facing forward. Unlike the Obi I was familiar with, this man didn't let his gaze wander or take in the wonder of the world around him.

My mind was having a difficult time reconciling the regal and confident Oberon to the pondering and snarky old man that I had befriended over the last year. *Why wear the mask of somebody else entirely instead of just changing your appearance?*

"Oh, Colette, I'm not so different from the friend you know. Obi is a persona I have taken on many times throughout the years. Nobody can stay mad at an old hermit after all. At most people simply write me off as strange and leave me to my business."

I flinched when he responded to my thoughts instead of my voice. I asked, "Wait, can you actually read my mind?"

He replied casually, as if we were discussing the weather. "Not exactly. Many Fae creatures have the ability to read surface level thoughts or to share memories with others. The title 'King of the Fae' isn't just for show; I can do everything my subjects can and more."

"Subjects?" I ask. "Besides Robin, who else do you rule over?"

Even his laugh was different as Oberon. Through a loud chuckle that seemed a touch rehearsed, Oberon replied, "Oh, all the Fae of the world, of course! Fairies like myself, pixies, dryads and nymphs, and so on. I'm honored to serve them."

Like the laugh, his response sounded forced. If I hadn't spent a year speaking to his alter ego I might not have noticed, but his perfect smile was plastered on his face instead of resting there like a real smile should. The tension around his eyes didn't look like someone who was smiling either.

A shiver went down my spine. His eyes still reminded me of the wolf hiding in the tree line that waited for me to turn my back before pouncing.

The trees continued to close behind us. I couldn't see the Court anymore behind us. Robin was floating a few feet behind us; just enough to keep himself in front of the collapsing path being left in our wake.

The home at the end of the path was an amalgamation. It had pillars, similar to the Court we left behind, but also arches of different shapes and sizes. There were at least six different designs of windows, and the roof was both short and tall depending on which half you looked at, with different sections being slanted or rounded or flat.

I turned my head on its side as if that would make the building in front of me make sense. Even with it being a random assortment of parts, it was still a beautifully crafted home. The wood shone as if freshly polished and the stone work looked completely new. It was . . . unique.

"Ah yes, my home is a bit confusing at first to all my friends that have visited over the years," Oberon started. He wrapped an arm around my shoulder, pulling me close, and started to point at specific features.

"Those pillars are from our time in Greece. We spent many years there. Many of those arch designs come from our time in Italy and France. Oh, and the lovely colored roofs come from our time in Spain. Titania was such a fan of their vibrant culture."

I shook my head and asked, "You took your house with you all across the world?"

Obi nodded sagely and replied, "Oh yes, of course. The Court would go where it was needed and bring us along with it so that we could be available to the Fae of the world. Titania and

I decided long ago that we would have our own space that we could bring along with us. She decided to make some interesting modifications at every stop we had."

That brought a smile to my face. I skipped up to the front steps and ran my hand along the smooth railing. It was a beautiful dark brown, similar to the surrounding trees. It was warm, somehow, and it felt more like home than anywhere I had ever been.

"It's incredible you were able to see all of those places," I said. "I would do anything to feel the breeze coming from a foreign shore. Or to smell the wonders of a marketplace completely new to me."

"Well, then, you simply must come inside," Oberon whispered in my ear, "because we have much to discuss."

Chapter Three

My head snapped back and forth, bouncing between looking at the crowded walls of the entryway and peeking through the various doorways that we walked past. Every inch of the wall housed a painting or a shelf with endless bits and bobbles. There were marble busts and statues of gold and silver and whole gemstones resting on the various pieces of ornately carved furniture.

"This way, my friend!" Obi exclaimed. "I am excited to show you how royalty dines."

I followed Obi through the hall with my eyes still raking over every detail of his home. I froze just short of entering the dining room. I was standing at a crossroads of the dining room in front of me and a sitting room to my left. My gaze was locked on a portrait hanging above the mantle.

Oberon was depicted in the portrait, in the same clothes he was wearing now. The woman next to him could only be his wife.

She was in a shining white dress wearing a crown of flowers. Her skin was fair and her hair was red like fire. There was a small smattering of freckles across her nose, which blended nicely with the comforting brown of her eyes. The smile on her face made me miss my mother.

"She is radiant, is she not?"

Oberon stopped back into the hallway to stand beside me. We stood there for more than a few minutes. I cleared my throat and replied, "Yes, she is so beautiful. Her eyes and her smile . . . they remind me of my mother." My hand idly pulled at a strand of my own fiery red hair.

Obi hummed in agreement and stated, "Like I told you before, you remind me of her. And not just because of your hair."

I gawked at him and flushed. It was a strange experience, being both confused and embarrassed, and I didn't like it.

He kept speaking before I could cut him off. "I was drawn to you because of your similarities. Your smile and your laugh warm people just like hers did. You are fiercely protective of your own heart and those you have given it to. I admire that you know that your love is precious, like she did."

"Most of all though, it's your passion for the world and its people. I always wanted to stay in one place and have a life with her. But Titania . . . she knew that the world needed to see how beautiful she was."

"Like I told you before, Colette. She was everything good in my life. Without her, I am a painting with color. A sky with no sun. If there was anything I could give to have her back, I would give it freely."

I let the tears flow freely down my face. I had no words or snarky remarks to throw back at my friend as he bared his heart to me.

Obi smiled softly at me before grabbing my hand and bringing me into the dining room. The table was covered in silver and gold serving dishes. He swept his arm out wide and gestured to a seat at one head of the table. "Have a taste of the world, Colette. As a token of our friendship," Oberon offered.

The number of foods, fruits, and pastries that I had never seen before made my stomach growl in anticipation. Robin scurried ahead of me to pull out my chair. There was already a place setting for me with a silk napkin.

Obi laughed as I quickly filled my plate with every dish I could reach. "No need to rush, Colette!" he boomed out between laughs. "Take your time. I will return shortly."

I grunted through a mouthful of warm pastry. The taste and smell of the food lulled me into a sense of bliss. I barely noticed as Robin pulled himself onto the corner of the table next to me.

He pointed frantically at the napkin that I had set aside in favor of filling my plate.

I giggled and teased, "Thank you for your concern, Robin, but I can handle myself. Would you like some?"

The fairy shook his head and snatched the pastry out of my hand. He tossed it back at me lightly. The cream filling spread across my cheek.

I gasped and jerked back in surprise. "Fine," I grumbled, "I'll use the napkin. Next time, just say it to me."

I unfurled the napkin and noticed that there were already smudges on its inside face. My eyes squinted to try to discern what the substance was. Fully opening the napkin and laying it across my lap, I read the words scrawled out in black ink and froze.

IN DANGER. RUN.

I looked back to Robin and whispered loudly, "What does this mean?"

Robin pointed back to the napkin and then pointed at the door intently.

I fought the urge to slam my head on the table. I pointed at my lips and said, "Use your words, Robin. Tell me what is wrong. Why do you think I'm in danger? I'm perfectly safe in my friend's home."

Robin pulled at his horns and opened his mouth as if to scream. No sound came out, but I imagine it would have been a groan.

I went to ask him another question but was stopped by the sound of footsteps coming down the stairs.

Robin's wings snapped up from their folded position and twitched to life. He ripped the napkin off my lap and balled it up in his fist before zipping out of the room.

Oberon walked back into the room holding a purple bottle in one hand and a wine cork in the other. "Hope you don't mind," he said, "but I wanted to grab something special to celebrate."

"Celebrate what?" I asked. My words came out scratchy and uneasy. I needed some of that wine to soothe my dry throat.

"Why, our friendship, of course!" Oberon laughed. He poured some wine into a glass chalice on the table. He handed it to me and added, "Spiced elven wine. Only the best for the king's guest."

It was a dark purple color at first, but as it swirled around my glass, I saw flecks of gold and silver. I shook myself out of my stupor and smiled fondly at Obi. "You don't have to do all of this, you know. Although it is appreciated," I said.

"Nonsense," Obi replied. "You deserve all of this and more. I'm just sorry it took so long to get here." He began piling food on his own plate, so I did the same.

We ate for over an hour. He shared stories about the different foods and where they were from. The wine was much better than anything I had ever had in the village. We laughed and talked and discussed all the places that I wanted to go. Every piece of silverware or bowl or picture on the wall had a story.

He promised to take me everywhere he had ever been.

Robin served us more wine and food throughout the night. He grabbed objects from other rooms to show to me. The entire time, he was trying to lock gazes with me. I ignored him and enjoyed the better company.

I never wanted it to end.

Several hours and a bottle of wine later, I was lying down on a borrowed bed in one of the many guestrooms of Obi's home. A stomach full of warm food and wine made it easy to accept the offer to stay the night. I drifted off to sleep in a matter of minutes.

"Puck! Get back here!"

I urged my wings to move faster. Master was so angry that I ruined his potion. I ducked between trees and through bushes to try to lose him, but he kept coming.

I burst into a clearing unexpectedly. He was too fast; he would catch me here! Pivoting on the spot, I dove back into the foliage and tried to double back.

A blow connected with my chest and sent me flying into the clearing. I skipped once on the hard ground before skidding to a stop. Trying to fly away, my wings gave out a few feet into the attempt. Before I could move again, Master's magic grabbed ahold of me and lifted me into the air.

"Puck! How dare you interfere with my wishes! You will be punished for this!"

The tears in my eyes clouded my vision. My ribs popped from the pressure of the magic binding me. "Master," I cried out, "Mistress would not have wanted this! What you are doing to these humans . . . it is more inhumane than any trick we ever pulled on them!"

Master dropped me into the dirt and placed his boot on my chest. "You used this arm," he whispered to me while grabbing my left wrist, "to betray me. You have lost the right to have it."

I screamed and tried to pull away, but his magic pressed down on me again. The force pushed me into the dirt. My screams turned to sobs and pleas as Master pulled my arm.

And pulled and pulled and *pulled*.

I rolled in the dirt screaming as I frantically tried to stop the bleeding from my now gaping shoulder wound. The pain when Master turned his magic into fire and cauterized the wound nearly made me faint.

I pleaded with my oldest friend, "Y-Your Majesty, please. I'm your f-friend. It's me, Puck."

"You are no friend of mine!" Master screamed, "Now you are just Robin Goodfellow, the fairy who grovels at the feet of the king. We are not friends."

Somehow, that almost hurt more than the burning injury on my side. I was truly alone again.

"And I wasn't finished, Robin. You betrayed me with your arm . . . and you also betrayed me with your voice. You are not worthy to even speak to me, whelp."

My eyes snapped open in time to see Master's hand, blazing with wild magic, reaching for my throat.

I let out one last wailing plea, "Master Oberon, no please! Spare me, spar—"

My scream of terror was silenced by the small, clawed hand of Robin. I was still in the guest bedroom of Oberon's house. My nightgown was drenched in sweat and I was panting as if I had been chased.

Puck sitting on a stool at my bedside. Tears were running freely down my face. I could still feel his terror. The feeling of betrayal as his oldest friend turned against him.

Crying alongside him, I pulled him into an embrace. His one arm tightened around me and we sobbed quietly together in the early morning light.

I pulled back and held him at arm's length. His scar tissue shimmered when I looked at it. I could still feel the heat from the fire and the pain from the . . . separation. I spoke quietly through my sobs, "Did all of that really happen to you? How did you show it to me?"

Puck backed out of my arms and pulled a small pad of paper out of his tunic's pocket. Using a piece of charcoal, he scratched something down and showed it to me.

MAGIC

"That really narrows it down, thank you. Why did he . . . do that to you? And what does he want with me?"

Puck closed his eyes in concentration and held out a hand. I took it and was bombarded with images and memories.

Titania's death, Oberon's mourning, his obsession with getting her back.

Oberon torturing and murdering other Far creatures with his magic. Sacrificing them?

He turned to kidnapping humans and trying to do the same. He learned that women similar to his wife would be necessary to bring her back.

He made a potion to prepare them for the ritual. Dark purple with hints of gold and silver. It took a year to brew.

He waited for them to sleep . . .

I snapped back into consciousness. Nausea flooded through my body and I threw up on the extravagant comforter that had been left for me. I felt Puck's little hand draw circles on my back.

"What do I do?" I whispered. My breaths came faster and faster as the walls inched closer toward me. Oberon was only two rooms down the hallway. *He was there waiting for the sun to finish rising so he could come and kill me. Sacrifice me?*

"Puck," I wheezed, "I don't understand what he wants. What do I do? What do I do?" My voice trailed off into an inaudible whisper. I gripped at the roots of my hair as if trying to pull the answer from my brain.

Puck's notepad slid into my field of view. He had erased his previous message and written a new one:

RUN

I shot out of bed and tore the nightdress off me. Puck pointed to a bundle of clothes in the corner, folded and clean from yesterday's journey. Fabric was pulled over my head quickly and without care. I couldn't tie the laces on my boots with my hands shaking so Puck had to do it for me.

Before I grabbed the door handle, I turned back to Puck. He was standing in the middle of the room nervously chewing on his thumb nail. I dropped to my knees and hugged him again. "Come with me," I said, "and you can stay with us. If you stay here, he'll kill you, Puck."

Puck shook his hand and gestured to the room around him. Pulling out his pad one last time he wrote:

HOME

A sobbed ripped its way out of me again at that. I smiled through the tears and stroked his hair. "Loyal to the end, Puck. You are an incredible friend."

He smiled back, all sharp teeth and acceptance, and bowed to me. He pushed me toward the door as more and more sunlight poured into the room from the window.

Grabbing the door knob, I turned it and stepped into the hallway.

Only to come face to face with the master of the house, Oberon.

Chapter Four

I begged my legs to move, but they were rooted firmly to the floor. My hands were suffering a similar fate; I couldn't stop them from forming tightly balled fists at my sides. The hallway was suffocating me with its imposing walls. All I could do was stare at the source of my fear.

Oberon stood in front of me with a concerned tilt of his head. He was holding a candle in one hand to guide him through the hallway. The little flame made me think of the fire he used to torture others. The dimly lit hallway made me think of the darkness that Puck tried to flee in.

We locked eyes and all I could think of was the wolf and its teeth and the blood—

"Colette? Why are you up so early?" Oberon asked.

The knot of nerves in my throat wouldn't let me respond. I coughed twice, one to clear my throat and one to give me courage. "G-Good morning, Oberon," I managed to squeak out, "I was just coming to find you, actually. My father will be worried about me so I really should be going."

His eyes dragged themselves down my body to inspect my traveling attire. "Ah," he spoke deliberately, "Well, I rather hoped we could travel some today, so it seems the edge of the woods will be the extent of our journey. Let me grab my coat and some boots before we leave."

I almost insisted that I could make the journey on my own but stopped myself at the last second. Instead, I said, "Of course. We can take a longer journey another time together, but I should let my father know where I was last night. I'll wait here for you."

We both paused for a long moment. My chest was so tight that it took all of my effort to keep myself standing. I kept my mouth shut tight so the thundering rhythm of my heartbeat wouldn't alert the predator in the room to my fear.

Oberon, seemingly satisfied with my answer, smiled and nodded at me. He turned and snuffed out the candle with a flick of his wrist.

"Wonderful!" he exclaimed over his shoulder. He walked a few steps before stopping and calling out to me again, "Oh, and did Puck bring you the glass of water this morning like I asked him to?"

"Yes, of course! Excellent service as always." The words tumbled out of my mouth before I could stop them. Only a few seconds after I spit my answer back at him did I realize what I had done.

There was a shift in the hallway; a pressure that hadn't been there before. It filled all the empty space around me and pressed down against my body. It felt like the pressure on a crossbow trigger just before a bolt was fired.

Oberon turned to face me. His green eyes were glowing now, and I had been right to fear them the other day. He had the eyes of the wolf on full display. I could see the hunger in his eyes. The madness.

"He told you then?" Oberon asked. It was a simple question.

It grated against my ears and made me clench my fists so hard that my nails dug into my palms. I shook my head up and down with tears clouding my vision.

A mirthless laugh from Oberon cut through the tension. "Well, I really am sorry about this, Colette," he whispered, "but it must be done."

The hallway switched from dim to vibrant in an instant. Oberon, snarling and yelling out some words I didn't understand, lunged at me. His hands were burning with the same blazing magic that he used to take Puck's voice.

I saw him diving for me in slow motion. His eyes a poisonous green, his teeth sharp and gritting together. He was only one step away now, and I couldn't move. I was stuck, horrified and waiting for him to use those vile hands to destroy me.

A blur of red, alight with its own pale pink and red magic, intercepted my attacker. Puck had launched a full body tackle at his master and used his own magic to knock him off course.

The impact of them slamming into the wall finally pulled me from my catatonic state. "Puck!" I screamed as they began to wrestle on the floor. Pictures and trinkets were falling off the wall and shattering on the floor.

Still channeling the surrounding magic, Puck grabbed a piece of debris and slammed it into the side of Oberon's head. He reeled back in surprise, and Puck used the opportunity to scurry out from underneath his master. Puck put himself in front of me with his fangs barred and one clawed hand ready to attack.

"Robin," Oberson growled, "You didn't learn your lesson last time, did you? How far you have fallen from my side."

Puck, unable to spit vitriol back at his old friend, shot me an intense look over his shoulder, and then flicked his eyes back down the hallway toward the entryway.

I nodded once with tears running freely down my face. Turning on my heel, I sprinted down the hallway. There was a scream of, "No!" from behind me followed by another impact of the two fairies.

All I could think of as I ran was how incredible of a friend Puck was. And how I left him to die at the hands of his torturer.

I burst through the front door of Oberon's home and continued my dead sprint into the woods. The easy pathway from before was gone, so I fought with branches and thorns to claw my way through the forest. They snapped and cut me without remorse.

I didn't know where I was going. The sun was slowly pulling itself above the horizon, but even with the morning light all I could see in any direction was a sea of dark oak trees.

I couldn't see the house anymore, but I felt the fury of Oberon's magic as he started to pursue me. It was like a heatwave that knocked the wind out of me. The sounds of the forest were gone and all I could hear was the forest behind me bending to its master's will.

The trees parted like water. I fell to my knees, surprised by the change, and turned back to see him.

Oberon, his house burning to the ground behind him, was standing with his arms spread wide. He had marks on his clothes and body, but there was no blood. His head was hung low, and it rose only with his heavy breathing.

My eyes stayed trained on him as I slowly rose to my feet. I took one step, then another, and managed to get a third step in before he snapped his eyes upward to lock with my own.

I broke into a sprint. He followed.

He was fast, and I only had a minute or two head start on him. I dove back into the tree line, but he simply parted the trees again.

I don't know how I stayed ahead of him, but I focused on running. Right, left, right, left, as fast as I could.

Right when I saw the Court come into view, I knew the only reason that I hadn't been caught yet was because I was being herded.

I ran between the pillars outside of the Court and dove behind one of them to take a second to breathe. Before I could peek around it to see where Oberon was, the pillar was blown apart as Oberon's arm thrusted through it to grab a fistful of my hair.

With a bloodthirsty cry, he heaved me across the floor by my hair. He pulled a scream from my throat along with my body as I skid across the broken tiles. My momentum added more cuts and gashes to my arms and face. I only stopped sliding once I collided with a stone bench near the middle of the Court.

Blood and tears dripping down my face, I could only watch as the King of Fairies swaggered toward me. His eyes—the wolf's eyes—were glaring down at me.

Oberon's hands flared again with magic as he ranted, "You should be thankful that your miserable life will forward my wishes, Colette. I am KING, and you should only be thankful that you had the chance to serve me."

I needed to reason with him, so I coughed out a response. "Please, Obi," I tried, "This is not what Titania would have wanted."

The crazed fairy appeared in front of me in a frightening burst of speed. He gripped the bench on either side of me, caging me in, and put his face a foot away from my own.

"Do not suggest what my queen would want, mortal," Oberon said through gritted teeth.

I had to try again, so I cried out, "She would be ashamed of you! If she knew you did these things . . . she wouldn't love you."

Deep within the swirling mass of malice and madness in his eyes, there was a sliver of grief; The grief was overwhelmed by his rage in a moment, but the feeling did not go unnoticed. Oberon ripped his head back to release a wordless cry to the heavens. The king jerked back, clawing at his hair as if to pull out his feelings of misery, and he yelled to the ruined halls around him,

"I am Oberon! King of the Fae Courts, Master of the Elements, Progenitor of the Seasons! I watched as forests were born and mountains climbed into the sky!"

His yell quickly turned into a startled sob. Unfamiliar tremors racked Oberon's body. He fought them, maybe like he had fought them before, but to no avail. The dam had burst.

I used both arms to pull myself up onto the bench. I saw him hunched over in pain as unwilling tears clawed themselves out of Oberon's eyes, his translucent wings twitching behind him in protest. One of his fingers touched a falling tear during his thrashing and he flinched back as if struck in the face.

My voice still scratchy from screaming, I said, "Even with all of those titles, you are still a grieving man. She is gone, Oberon, and it is okay to feel lost. Everyone does when they lose the most important thing in the world to them."

Oberon threw both hands skyward, making a fist with each of them, and pulled, as if trying to bring the clouds down to have an audience with him. The sky somehow understood his command, and the Court became the target of a torrential downpour.

Hair matted like a wild animal's and with tears now masquerading as raindrops, the king snarled at me and raged, "I do not *feel* as you do, mortal. I do not cry, and I do not mourn. Titania *will* return to me once I have found her favor again. I don't care if it takes your life or a thousand more. I will have my queen again!"

The gripping fear in my chest had gone numb now. I found the strength to stand in the freezing rain, so I dug deeper and found the strength to scream, "Then where is she, oh Great King? Have you not killed enough innocent Fae and friends of yours to find her? Did you not butcher your oldest and most loyal friend, Puck, in your rage? Have you not seen what a monster you have become in her absence?"

Oberon approached me again, and the fear returned in full force. I tripped over the bench and hissed as I cut my arms and back on more broken tiles during my fall. He loomed over me like a shadow, glaring down at me.

"I am no monster," he replied, "Just a king without his queen. Take honor in knowing you will assist in returning her to me."

I felt dizzy. My vision was becoming clouded with black clouds forming at its edges. I locked my gaze to Oberon's rage-filled visage and my hands grasped at the slick tile floor beneath me.

The grief was prominent in his eyes now. It would continue to consume him long after his madness consumed me. I threw myself upward, blood and rainwater trailing behind me, and unclenched my fist just enough to the jagged tip of a stone shard peeked through my fingers. Not expecting an assault, Oberon caught the almost six-inch-long stone shard in the side of his neck.

The rain stopped. The sun, the clouds, every leaf, and every creature halted to watch how the fate of the Fae King would unfold.

"Did you think it would be that easy?" Oberson asked with calm indifference. "Colette, I am immortal. You have no hope of killing me."

I stood, rigid as a status, holding the shard firmly in his neck. My vision was darkening again. All I could see were his eyes now.

"How did Titania die then?" I asked to stall for time. I needed to think. I needed to think.

"She surrendered her immortality to better understand you stupid mortals. A foolish mistake."

"Didn't you say you would give her anything?"

Oberon blinked one, surprised, and I felt just the same. The words had flown out of my mouth before I could catch them. He laughed, a true laugh, before grabbing my wrist.

"I will admit, Colette, it is hard to surprise me," Oberon said with a smile, "but the impudence of humans never ceases to do just that."

"Wait," I pleaded. "Why struggle for years and years trying to find a way to bring her back, when you could see her now? Instead of fighting to have another moment with her, why not be with her forever, right now?"

I smiled at him with the taste of blood on my tongue, and managed to gargle out, "After all, death is simply the final journey we all must take, right? That's what you told me."

My grip on my makeshift weapons came loose as my vision went black.

C olette collapsed in front of me. Soaking wet and covered in blood, the beautiful girl was reduced to a shallow breathing corpse-to-be. Her hair, flaming like the rays of the morning sun, were splayed around her on the ground like a halo.

It seems that her wounds were too much for her. I felt a pang of regret, a foreign feeling, at the loss of such a wonderful life. The world would be less bright without her.

I smiled down sadly at her, still fascinated at the fact that mortals could continue to surprise me. Grabbing the stone shard in my neck I ripped it out with only a hole in my neck to show for its efforts.

I whispered to the winds of the mortal plane, "I knew I was right when I said you were just like Titania, Colette. Only she could convince me to do something as insane as this."

And I let go.

A trickle of blood rolled out of my neck wound, followed by another, and another. Before I could change my mind, I let the pain overtake me.

I fell to my knees, grinning with a combination of gnashing teeth and blood, and spoke my final promise,

"I'm coming, Titania. Just another moment, and I will be there."

Like strings cut from a puppet, I fell limp besides the rapidly cooling Colette.

I'm coming, my love.

About the Author

C hristian Carter is a new author who has enjoyed writing since his teen years. He enjoys high fantasy and science fiction with his absolute favorite genre being dystopian fiction. A personal favorite of his is Paulo Coehlo's *The Alchemist*.

Christian is thankful for the opportunity to write and publish this story with a wonderful cast of coauthors. While this is his first published work, he has been both inspired and encouraged by the opportunity. He is excited to continue working on his dystopian novel *Clouds of Ash* as well as an anthology of fantasy short stories.

The Nightmare

M.D. Casmer

E very time Ryan Wheatley tried to blink away the nightmare that morning, he saw the figures slithering and intertwining their shapeless appendages. Was it one figure or multiple? He couldn't tell. Trying to figure it out triggered a primal instinct to look away. To find light and hide within its shelter from the darkness and the monsters.

He had spent an eternity in that space between existence in his dreams the night before. It hadn't felt like a dream. Ryan somehow understood words that human mouths couldn't form, and the secrets they told him made him want to curl up into a ball and cry until it was all over.

Try as he might, he couldn't remember them after he woke up. The only thing he could remember was an understood promise. That if he, Ryan Wheatley, went back to them, he would be theirs.

Every time his eyes closed, they were there waiting for him as if just outside a window that looked into his room. Or was it Ryan who was on the outside and peering in? The dream was so realistic, yet waking up felt the same as it always had, like a new day.

Ryan got out of bed, deciding that coffee might help the lingering nightmare go away. The wonderful aroma filled his kitchen as he began making the coffee. In spite of the nightmare, or perhaps because of it, he appreciated the savory scent of the coffee as it brewed on his counter in the glass carafe. He allowed his mind to quiet as he followed the morning ritual of manually making his coffee.

Set water to boil in the kettle.

Grind coffee to a medium-coarse texture.

Add filter to top of pour-over carafe.

Use the preheated water to rinse the filter.

Return...

Ryan stopped. He had to think for a moment about what it was that he was supposed to be returning to. The nightmare crossed his mind, and the coaxing croon of the impossible speech. *It might not be a bad idea to go back,* Ryan thought. *Better to side with them now, instead of forcibly when it isn't his choice.*

He froze in place as he realized the thoughts weren't his. Something else had put those thoughts in his head.

Pain brought Ryan back to his surroundings. His hand was an angry red from the hot water that had spilled over the lip of the carafe. He hadn't stopped pouring from the kettle.

With a yelp that could have come from someone half his size, Ryan continued his coffee routine, placing the kettle back on the stove with fresh water and minimal swearing. He quickly cleaned up the mess and continued where he left off.

Ryan added the grounds to his filter and swirled them to cause a small divot in the middle to accept the water. All that was left for him to do was to wait for the water to boil again, then cool for a minute or two. Usually, this ended up timing perfectly so that Ryan didn't have to break his concentration. Now that he had a few minutes before he could finish making his morning coffee, he pulled out his phone and checked his work emails.

It was still too early in the morning for any activity to start for the day, so he switched to social media and scrolled through the numerous posts that refreshed constantly.

Dogs, cats, dances, author promos, conspiracy theories, and more danced around his thoughts, and he could feel his still sleepy eyes strain at the screen. He turned off the screen, set it on the counter, and rubbed at his temples to relieve the seed of a headache forming.

Make the choice. Return. Be with Barbybauighlbubblaggl.

Ryan's eyes flared open. He was face down on the counter, slumped against the cabinets. The water was bubbling invitingly, inches from his face. The smooth and cool countertop stuck to his cheek slightly as he peeled himself to a standing position.

It must have been the water boiling that he heard mixing with the nightmare. Or was that part of the language that he could somehow understand in his sleep? A name perhaps? It seemed alien to him now and was very obviously the sound of boiling water and not him having a mental break.

Ryan finally returned to his coffee process, finishing it and drinking in the smell of freshly brewed coffee. It was almost better than the taste of the stuff itself. Almost. That first sip always reminded him why he practiced the mindfulness of the process. The connection with his drink made the payoff satisfying both to his palate as well as to something deeper inside himself.

Sleepiness faded from him as if being fended off with a torch like a wild animal. At least, as effectively as torches seemed to work in movies that Ryan had watched. He logged in to work early to keep his mind active and settled in for an excruciatingly long Monday. He tried as hard as he could to tell himself that he was merely overtired and that nothing weird was going on at all.

Sounds of writhing flesh on a slick floor echoed off a dark, starless void. Turning around, Ryan found himself standing in a cave, gazing out into the shifting colors between stars that led to nowhere. Vertigo started to encroach on his senses, and he felt unsteady as the slimy stone-like surface beneath him grew around his ankles, keeping him in place. It didn't help his dizziness, though.

The cave walls came into focus as his eyes adjusted to the darkness. They shifted when his eyes slid over them, unable to take in the detail yet recognizing its sturdiness. It was the stone around his ankles that helped him identify what was going on.

Stone tendrils lashed around him as they slowly, almost unnoticeably, crept up toward his knees. At least, 'stone' was the texture he could best describe.

It reminded him of the boulders beneath a waterfall that his parents had taken him to as a kid. The slick surface of the cave was made only more slippery by the growth that clung to its not-quite-rock faces. The connection clicked the rest of the cavern into focus, now that his mind had a way to grasp what he was seeing.

The walls and floor were twisting on itself. The cave wasn't a solid rock depression in a mountain. It was a mass of smaller tendrils nestling together as it swelled and shrank in places. It created the enclosure he was standing in. It was wrapping around him tighter and higher.

Managing to turn enough to see down the cavern, Ryan could make out its depths. Or rather, lack thereof. Behind him, where a normal cave might go deeper, was a concave black orb. It absorbed the minuscule light from the stars outside that had caused Ryan to believe the cave had gone deeper.

It was an eye.

He could feel it tracing him, watching him in ways he didn't understand. It was observing things that would cause Ryan pain to try to comprehend.

You've returned.

The voice thundered in his head, and he screamed in pain.

"No, no, no," was all Ryan was able to whimper.

Ryan's phone vibrated against his face. The sun was up now, and he had fallen asleep on his keyboard. Dozens of pages with nothing but the continuous letter 'j' filled a report he was working on.

He found that his feet got tangled in the cables of his work computer. It took a considerable amount of care and coordination to get out of them without unplugging his computer and losing his open work. Not to mention it would show him as offline. He was already a few strikes too many to show any blips in his 'work ethic.'

Once free, he saw a flashing orange notification on his work calendar. He was an hour late for a meeting.

"Fuck!" He scrambled back into his chair and began sending a message to his boss. The meeting might still be going on, if he was lucky.

His phone buzzed again, an incoming call from his boss. Ryan groaned at what he knew was going to be an uncomfortable call.

"Hello?" Ryan said after he mustered up the courage to answer. Luckily, he managed it before the call went to voicemail.

"Return to me. Fulfill the pact—"

Ryan screamed and dropped the phone. It hit the floor and went dark. It was the voice from the thing in his dreams. The thing in the cave—no, that wasn't right. It *was* the cave. It had spoken to Ryan while he was awake. Or was he still in a dream?

As soon as his phone turned on after being plugged in, it began to buzz again. This time, he was ready for the voice. He would ask it what it wanted. Why it needed Ryan to 'return.'

He answered.

"Yo, Ryan, where are you? You missed the check-in, and it was your turn to present. Are you on PTO today?"

"Actually, yeah," Ryan lied as relief flooded through him. "I was drafting an email to tell you I needed a sick day. Turns out it's worse than I thought. I'm headed to urgent care for some meds to help. I should be back online tomorrow."

His boss understood. He usually did. But there is only so much understanding a boss can do before their hands are tied and they have to invite you to no longer show up for work. Ryan knew that firsthand. Unfortunately, that had happened more than once.

Despite the chipper demeanor, Ryan noted the rigid, professional tone.

Ryan needed to figure out what was going on with these dreams. They left him feeling shaken and cold every time he woke up, and he was even more tired than he was before. Maybe he actually was getting sick.

He remembered that horrible eye.

The voice that he shouldn't be able to understand.

The slithering mass of flesh that wound up his knees.

A clatter sounded at the door, and Ryan's eyes came back into focus, fear freezing him in his seat.

A deep breath.

Another.

Nothing happened.

Slowly, Ryan got up, careful to make as little noise as possible. Moving across his living room, from where his work computer and gaming computer were set up for convenience, Ryan tucked close to the wall. He grabbed the first thing he came across to use as a weapon if needed.

Ryan was in the corner of the room, just on the side of the doorway. If he looked around the edge, he would see whatever clattered into his house. He just had to do it.

Better to get it over with. *Man up, Ryan!* he thought to himself.

Turning the corner, he screamed and swung his umbrella in the empty space that was his entryway , hoping to batter the nightmare into submission, or at least enough to get away.

Mail sat on the floor.

It had been the mail slot. Ryan laughed in relief. He turned to go back to his desk and found himself staring directly into the giant eye again. It made quick and jerky movements while watching things that cannot be seen from a place that cannot be fathomed by a mortal mind. As Ryan looked into it, it focused on him.

R yan woke up in his dark bathroom. His throat was raw, as if he'd been screaming, and his hands hurt. He didn't remember falling asleep. He didn't even remember coming into the bathroom. The only thing he could remember was that misshapen, concave eye. It had no iris and pupil, as it was all the same color, or lack thereof. In its place was a slight protrusion that moved as if something was crawling around under a blanket. The shape of it shifting back and forth toward whatever it was focusing on.

Ryan didn't know how he knew, but he could feel when it was focusing on him.

He shook himself after a while, trying to forget the image. How long had he been here? He could feel that he was hungry but was uninterested in eating. Had he eaten with his coffee earlier? Why did his hand hurt so badly?

He flicked on the light and found writing smeared on his walls. Symbols and drawings covered every flat surface of the bathroom. Out of the corner of his eye, they appeared to be English letters, maybe even words. But when he focused on them and tried to read them, they turned into meaningless scratches and squiggles.

His hands were covered in ink and blood from deep cuts on his palms. He found broken, and in some cases chewed, pens and markers pushed to the corners of the room.

Turning to the mirror, he saw that it was cracked and spider-webbed from a point level with his own face. That explained the cuts on his hand.

He moved around the distorted fractures to examine himself. He had smears of blood on his face, along with smudged ink and scratches. His hair was disheveled, which was normal, but it unnerved him all the same. His skin had gone paler than it ever had in Ryan's life, and his eyes had joined in the party, going to a blue so dull that it was almost white.

But there was something worse in that broken mirror.

He could read the words on the walls.

Spinning around, he found the strange squiggles and shapes just as unreadable as before. Ryan turned back to the mirror and found that he could read them again as easily as if they were notes he'd taken. They were even in his own handwriting.

The only problem was that the words made no sense together. He didn't know what order they were supposed to be read in.

Return, the multitone voice said. It seemed to come from everywhere. It wasn't that it was loud — it was thunderous. The presence of it was staggering.

Return.

Ryan screamed, trying to let the pain in his throat fill his entire mind, and push out the intruder and feel something other than helplessness. He spun and punched the wall, right where one of the glyphs that resembled the eye was.

It was gone.

Ryan's fist shattered through the drywall before he could pull it back. White dust puffed out onto the clean floors. He stood in disbelief, surveying his bathroom.

Moments before, it was covered in symbols and squiggles and drawings that evoked terror and uneasiness. Some even moved places when he'd studied them. But now it was the same bathroom he'd always had.

Ryan glanced at his hand again. Despite being covered in white dust from the wall, and a scrape from nicking a stud in the wall, there weren't any other wounds on his hand.

He turned back around. The mirror was intact. No spiderwebbing crack. No blood from where his hand pressed into it. Nothing. It was as if he'd imagined it all.

Ryan swore that he didn't imagine it all. It was there. It *had* to have been there. It had been there before he screamed. Was he losing control of what was real and what wasn't?

Ryan sat down on the edge of his bathtub and began to cry.

Deciding the best course of action now was to take a shower, Ryan did so and put on fresh clothes. He kept moving by doing busywork around the house. Dishes, vacuuming, going through his mail, anything he could find. Staying occupied kept his mind off the . . . well, the things he'd rather not think about at that moment. If he thought about them, he might see it again. If he saw it again, he might *return*. Best left for when he could get himself together. Then he'd figure out how to get rid of it. Ryan lived by the philosophy that you couldn't sort out any issues if you didn't have yourself sorted out first.

The only problem that Ryan had after finishing everything he could find to put his hands to work, was that his home was spotless. He'd even put his remote control and gaming controllers in a neat line on his coffee table. Which meant he was running out of things to do. His belly rumbled, and he was relieved to have found something else to do.

The sun was going down and Ryan had emptied his fridge to find whatever ingredients he had that weren't wilted or sludge from neglect and a love of pizza. He was going to attempt to make a stir-fry , macaroni and cheese, and cheesecake. At least, that's what he'd hoped they would turn out as. Ryan wasn't known among his friends as the handiest in the kitchen.

Everything was going well through the stir-fry , but it wasn't until he pulled another pot out to start the mac and cheese that something twinged his senses. He was acutely aware for the first time in his own home how his kitchen was positioned. His back was facing the empty rooms that only grew darker with the setting sun. And something was watching him.

The small hairs on the back of his neck stood on end. Ryan's movements became jerky and forced in the way that only pretending not to notice something can make happen. It seemed to come from the same spot in his brain that shut off whenever someone asked him what his favorite song was. Ryan focused on picking up any sounds that would give away his spectator. The scuff of a step, the swish of legs walking. Maybe even the creak of the floorboards as weight shifted. He needed something to identify that it wasn't his nerves playing tricks on him.

He found his opportunity as he reached for a spoon to stir. Time slowed for Ryan. His heartbeats thundered in his ears as the anticipation rose. He didn't know what he would do if his paranoia was validated.

Would he run?

No. If something was deft enough to break in and watch, Ryan wasn't sure he could escape it. He got winded if he took the laundry from the basement all the way to his bedroom on the second floor.

Would he attack it?

That thought was almost as laughable to him as running.

Ryan found that he just needed to know. Was it an intruder? Or was it the eye calling for him? Whatever it was that was begging for him to return?

Time sped back up to normal, and Ryan whipped around to scan the living room behind him. His injured hand smacked into the cabinet beside him, sending an angry surge of pain. But he noticed nothing in the room out of the ordinary.

To be sure, he mustered up the courage to walk into the room ready to confront his fears head-on.

H is living room hadn't seemed that dark from the kitchen. Ryan felt around the room for a light switch to turn on the lamps. He brushed the smooth walls with his fingertips, hoping to come across it. He knew it had to be nearby, as he'd done this countless times before.

The smooth walls slowly transitioned from the painted drywall of his living room into the slick, lumpy, squirming wall that instantly made him feel clammy and queasy. Ryan pulled his hand back as if bitten by something. He turned back and didn't see his kitchen anymore. Rather, he saw that shifting swirl of deep blues, purples, and endless black dotted by unfamiliar stars in shapes that were too intentional to be random from the mouth of the cave that opened to the infinite.

His breath became ragged, and as he turned to peer back down the cavern, into the eye that he knew had been watching him in his kitchen, he realized he couldn't. His legs were locked together by the stony tendrils that had wrapped around his legs again. They came up higher than his ankles this time—they were up to his waist. He couldn't pivot or turn without losing his balance. He could feel them grasping higher up his body, accompanied by the wet smacking sounds of their writhing and twisting. Whatever it was, it wanted him to look out into the nothingness of what Ryan somehow knew to be everything.

You've returned.

A hand emerged from the void beyond the lip of the cave, grasping the edge. A figure pulled itself into view, standing in the way of Ryan and his only hope of exit from the eye that he knew was focusing on him from the back of the cave.

"No," was all Ryan managed to whimper in protest.

The form had no legs. It was a torso that sprouted from the tendrils that made up the cavern he stood trapped in. A long torso made of knots topped with what resembled arms that bent at wrong places, shoulders that creaked and shifted position up and down the torso, and a head. The head had tips of tendrils sticking out of it where the knots ended. There was a depression that bubbled similarly to muscles that flexed against one another as it spoke, in place of a proper mouth. The single eye of the creature was the same as the eye in the cavern, mere inches behind Ryan. It moved forward, tendrils whipping up into existence from those that made up the cave to join the body, pulling it forward as tendrils exited the back of it, becoming one with the cave. As it grew closer, Ryan could see that the whole body was made of the interlocking cavern tendrils.

It reached for him with misshapen hands, uttering sounds in multiple pitches that he knew were syllables to words that didn't make sense to his ears but resonated with fear in his mind.

Ryan screamed and resisted his restraints, pulling at them as effectively as trying to rip a brick out of a wall with only his fingertips. He pushed with his legs against the floor, feeling the shifting cavern beneath him. He was able to leverage himself enough, push just enough with his legs, to pull on the little purchase he could get with his fingers. A single tendril loosened enough for him to twist.

He was able to twist and trip out of the grasp of the cavern's grip. He stumbled, preparing for the impact into the great concave eye behind him.

Ryan felt his face hit the wooden floorboards of his kitchen.

R yan flipped over on the floor and crab-walked into the kitchen, his eyes searching his empty living room for the reaching . . . thing.

All he saw was his computer sleep screen transitioning through different night sky pictures, softly illuminating a small part of the now dark room. The silence here was deafening compared to that cave in space. Quiet here meant that he could still hear the fans of that computer, fans from his air conditioning kicking on and off, traffic driving by his house on the street. This non-quiet was comforting. He couldn't hear his heartbeat echo off the walls, or the sound of a panicked swallow go all the way down to his stomach. He couldn't hear his stomach digesting whatever he ate with his coffee earlier that day.

Ryan's mind was jolted to life at the thought of food. He flipped around and saw smoke billowing from the stir-fry pan, and the water was boiling over from the pot next to it. Flames sputtered and spat in response to the scalding water. A different kind of panic, a panic that he could do something about, knotted in his chest, and he launched to his feet and shut off his stove. Throwing away the last of his now inedible groceries in the trash.

The sense of accomplishing something, even though it wasn't ideal to have to accomplish in the first place, calmed Ryan down. It was a tangible goal that made sense, one that he could achieve. That sense of perspective allowed him to untie some of that cloud of confusion that had been hanging around his mind all day, or at least what he could remember of the day.

Ryan couldn't remember where he'd been or what he'd done for large swathes of time. He remembered making coffee, working a little bit, and cleaning the bathroom. But that all couldn't have made up more than a handful of hours together.

He also remembered everything from the nightmare. The eye, the creature, the cave, the void, the tendrils—all of it. Ryan realized that he'd spent most of the day in that nightmare, and he put it together.

The voice wanted him to return to sleep. To the cavern. To the eye.

Ryan vowed to himself that he would do whatever it took to stay awake until he could figure out how to get rid of the nightmare.

He did the next logical step he could think of.

He ordered an extra-large pizza and several bottles of the most caffeinated soda to go with it, then pulled out his old coffee machine and brewed a pot. He wasn't going for quality stimulants anymore, so that ruled out the pour-over method. He was going for quantity.

T he police cruiser pulled up to the small, dark house.

"Yeah, we just got here. Going to knock and see if anyone's home," the driver said.

"You want me to go with you?" the passenger cop asked, his eyes locked on a game he was playing on his phone.

"Nah, should only be a minute. Either he answers, or he's not home. Whichever one it is, it'll only take a minute. Then I'll kick your ass in the next round while we wait for our next dispatch."

The driver got out and walked up to the house, pulling his flashlight out to illuminate the door in the autumn night. He knocked with the butt end of the flashlight and called out.

"Police! Anyone home?"

The cop waited on the porch for a few long minutes before reaching out to push the doorbell and knock again.

The door flew open and a deranged man with chalk-white skin and what looked to be deep bruises around his eyes stared at him from a crouch.

"You can't take me back. I'll never return, you hear me?! *I'LL NEVER RETURN!*" Ryan slammed the door in the cop's face so hard that it bounced back open. The police officer could hear him screaming and cackling through the house.

The officer signaled for his partner, and they entered the house together. They kept their lights up and cleared the entryway.

The living room appeared as if a squatter had lived there for years. It smelled like it too. Trash littered the floor, stuffing was ripped from the furniture, and a campfire had been made in the middle of the floor at some point in the last few days. The smoke coated the walls of the living room, and drawings seemed to leak onto the walls from the doorway at the back.

Stairs to the left led to an upper level of the house, and the walls had been scored with what resembled scratch marks. The first officer was hoping he could convince his partner to go up and check it out instead of him. When his partner moved to go up automatically, as they were trained, he sighed a little in relief.

"Mr. Wheatley, we're with the police department. We just want to make sure you're doing alright. Can you come out so we can speak?" he called.

A rattling came from the closed door in the back of the room. It sounded like dishes clanking together.

The officer moved carefully toward the door, his eyes locked onto it and his hand on his gun, just in case.

A crunching sound came from beneath the officer's boot. He paused and the rattling behind the door stopped. It was a crudely carved figure that had long spiky arms and no legs. Brown splotches covered it that the officer identified as possible blood.

He waited as still as he could muster, even holding his breath.

"Mr. Wheatley? I just want to talk. Folks are worried about you. Nobody's been able to reach you since Monday. That's five days ago. It's Saturday, Mr. Wheatley."

A wailing came from behind the door, and it flew open. Ryan Wheatley was sobbing as he crawled toward the officer and threw his arms around his legs.

"Help me, I can't go back. I *won't* go back!" Ryan sobbed as he thumped his head with a fist full of chewed and ripped nails.

When the cop looked down to meet the man's eyes, they were black.

They weren't gone, but they absorbed the light from his flashlight and stood out in stark contrast. A faint swirling could be seen within them, maybe shades of blue and purple.

Then Ryan's head collapsed on the officer's boots, his arms falling heavily to the ground.

He appeared to have passed out.

It was only a handful of seconds from stepping on the figurine to Mr. Wheatley falling into a deep, death-like sleep at his feet. His partner flew down the stairs after it had all happened, firearm drawn.

"Everything okay?" he asked.

"Yeah," the first officer said. "His eyes were strange, though. Can you help me take a look?"

Even closed, Ryan Wheatley's eyes appeared to be bruised. Further inspection of his face found other bruises and a split lip, as if he'd been beating himself. It made sense, as the house appeared to be empty, and he witnessed the young man punching himself only moments before.

The partner officer opened an eyelid and flashed his light in Ryan's eye. It rolled to the back of his head, but it was brown and normal.

"You say they looked weird? Apart from the fact that he looks like he went twelve rounds with Rocky?" the partner asked.

"Must have been a trick of the light," the officer said. His heart was still racing from Ryan bursting through the kitchen door.

Now that he was calming down, he was feeling tired from the spike of adrenaline.

The two police officers carried Ryan Wheatley to the ambulance that had arrived in short order.

The first officer yawned. "You think you can drive us to the next call? I need a nap. The creepiness took it out of me."

"Yeah, no problem," his partner said. They switched sides, got in the car and took off.

They drove away into the night, and the officer fell asleep almost instantly in the passenger seat, dreaming of Ryan Wheatley's eyes.

About the Author

M.D. Casmer, a Metro-Detroit native, spends his free time in fictional worlds and galaxies that he created or in his woodshop making dust and swearing loudly. While not normally a horror writer, his addition to this collection has made him reconsider its standing in his literary pursuits. To find and contact M.D. Casmer, you can visit his website and blog at or on social media with his username being "mdcasmer" on all platforms.

List of Contributors

Brandee Paschall
Brig Berthold
Christian Carter
Ciar Pfeffer
Emma Jane Lounsbury
Kelly Virens
M.D. Casmer
Maile Starr
Nelle Nikole

Playlist

S can the QR code or follow the link below to listen to the Crumpled Papers and Empty Caskets playlist on Spotify!

SCAN FOR SPOTIFY

qrco.de/beLk40

Made in the USA
Middletown, DE
03 November 2023

41759251R10166